YOUNG WYTCH

Book One in the Isfael Series

Wilbur Seymore

ISBN – 9798363192685

Life is a rich tapestry that we weave through our interactions, and each of us has a yarn to spin. History is the picture we see when looking back.

CONTENTS

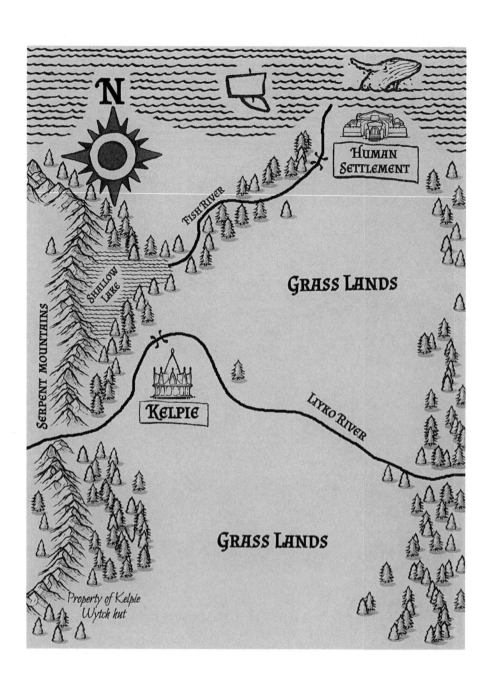

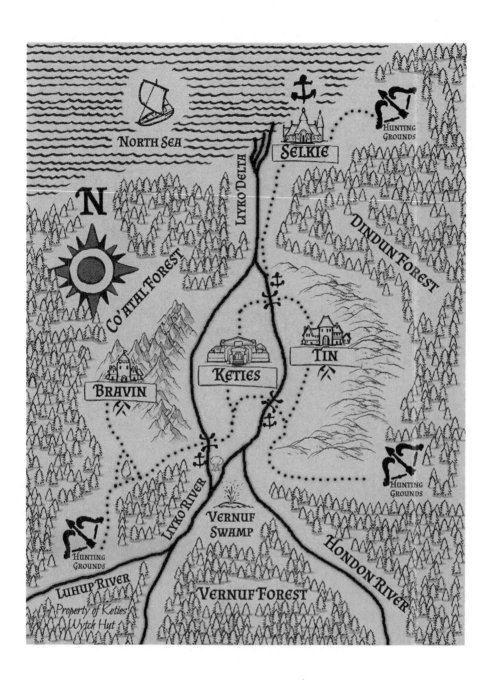

HUNT

Cold winds roll in from the northeast, herding thick grey clouds across the sky, whilst a bleak sun tries its best to shine light on the world. Tree branches rocked by the flow of air shed their autumn colours so that they may close in on themselves and ride out the coming winter.

A herd of fallow deer sloth their way through the dense groundcover. They keep raising their heads at the slightest noise to check for danger and pull their ears back to listen for predators sneaking up behind them.

Hunkered down in the thick band of bracken ferns that crowd the edge of the clearing is a huntress whose light brown eyes watch the animals scavenge for food. A fine woollen net stops her braided hair from swatting her in the face as the wind dances through the forest. Wrapped around her waist is a heavy leather belt that bears the tools of her trade, each item held firmly by strips and twine so she can move silently through the dense woods in this game of survival.

The huntress holds a small recurve bow made of goat horn, and a nocked arrow rests securely on her index finger. Checking the sway of the branches, she can tell that the wind is favourable.

She looks over to her left. Her husband has taken up a position behind a pile of rocks, his hunting spear held low to avoid alerting the animals. A simple nod of the head indicates that he is ready. Isfael returns the gesture and picks a target.

The chosen animal is an old doe flicking through the thick

leaf mat in search of something edible. Isfael waits until the deer presents itself broadside to allow for an uninterrupted shot at the killing spot, a hand-sized target low down on the chest, just behind the arm roast.

As the female elf rises up on one knee to clear the ferns while drawing her bow and focusing on the target, the doe stops grazing and raises its head to look directly in huntress's direction. Isfael tilts the tip of her draw thumb out and away from her middle finger ever so slightly by pushing it forward, allowing the string to slip over the polished surface of the bronze thumb ring and give flight to the missile.

It's a perfect shot that pierces the animal's ribcage. Fright and surprise send the doe leaping up into the air with the arrow still stuck in her flank, which startles the rest of the herd and sends them fleeing deeper into the forest, followed by the wounded animal.

Isfael bursts out of her hiding spot and sets off after her quarry, slipping her bow over her shoulder and pulling out her bronze mattock all in one smooth motion. Her husband, who joins in the chase, soon leads the way.

The pursuit is over quickly.

A wail rolls through the woods, a distressed moan which speaks on the fear of the encroaching death. The male hunter moves past the dying animal and immediately begins a chant to activate his talent.

Isfael nears the doe and delivers the killing blow by slamming the blade of her mattock into the base of the deer's skull to sever the spine. Then she kneels down, brushes some leaves out of the way and picks up a pinch of soil which she rubs into the animal's fur. 'I thank you for your sacrifice, noble beast. Your soul is free to return to Mother Nammu. Walk amongst your ancestors with pride.'

After having completed his sweep of the area to make sure that there isn't any danger in the immediate vicinity, Yelqen props his spear up against a tree and addresses her. 'That was an impressive shot. One hundred and seventy paces, was it?'

Isfael wipes the blood off her mattock, stows it away and takes out her skinning dagger. Then she spins her thumb ring over so that its long smooth lip faces outwards. 'Yes, I would say it was around that distance.'

As she pulls the arrow shaft free of the carcass she notices that its head has come unstuck. 'Hope the tip hasn't broken.'

'I'm sure the Master Fletcher won't mind retipping your arrow,' Yelqen remarks while taking the rope out of his backpack, remaining alert to the surrounding forest. 'I'm just hoping that the brown bear who lives in these parts will stay back until we're finished...' He drops the rope and retrieves his spear. 'Ah, and here comes Old Beggar. As if summoned!'

A large male bear saunters through the trees, heading straight for the two elves. Each exhalation releases a cloud of vapour that envelopes his head and shoulders.

Yelqen places himself between the beast and his wife. He can see that the animal is already fairly plump so it might be less likely to attack, but he is not taking that chance. 'Good day to you, cousin.'

The bear stops and sniffs the air when he hears the greeting. He slowly sits down and watches the elven pair.

Isfael leaves the security to her husband while she works on the carcass; years of hunting have allowed her to hone her skills, making the removal of the organs a simple task. 'Dammit, this does not look promising.' She cuts the heart open and pulls out the pieces of flint. 'Arrow tip has snapped in half, must've clipped a rib on the way in.'

Yelqen is still facing the bear. 'Can we go yet? Old Beggar here is getting restless.'

'Almost done.' Isfael makes little slices in all of the organs. 'I just need to do a parasite check.'

Suddenly the bear gets on all fours and begins approaching the couple.

'No!' Yelqen raises his voice and lowers his stance. He holds the spear out before him, ready to thrust. 'Back!'

Isfael immediately stops working and gets into a defensive

pose, ready to fight. Old Beggar stops with a huff and paws at the ground. Seeing that the situation has calmed for now, she quickly finishes up by tying a rope around the doe's feet and calling her husband over.

Very slowly Yelqen backs away from the bear while keeping the animal in sight. Drawing level with his wife, he hands his spear over and draws out his palstave axe. Isfael take the shaft weapon and slides it through the ropes on the deer's feet. Together they lift the carcass off the ground and begin backing away, making sure to keep their eyes on the bear at all times while holding their axes at the ready.

Old Beggar walks over to the pile of organs and begins to eat, signalling to the two elves that it is relatively safe to turn around and leave.

At the edge of their hunting grounds they stop by a totem pole where they lay the carcass down to take a break. Both elves are dressed in short linen skirts that stop just above the knee and long-sleeved shirts which allow their bellies to show. Their attire has been dyed a dark brown simply because it is the most readily available colour in their part of the world. Soft leather shoes stuffed with dried grass stop their toes from going numb with cold. The clothing they have chosen to wear might not be the best for retaining heat, but it does allow for greater mobility during the hunt.

Yelqen removes his pack and empties it; each item is placed on a blanket after having passed his inspection. Amongst the pack's contents are a pair of woven cloaks as well as double-layered linen trousers which he lays out on the blanket to air them out. 'I'll be glad to get these on. The wind is biting today.'

Isfael briefly looks over her shoulder and makes a sound of agreement as she approaches the totem. She is counting the pegs protruding from the intricately carved rock pillar. 'We're the last couple out. Same as always.'

Yelqen whistles to regain his wife's attention and chucks a wooden peg in her direction; the large dowel has their names engraved on it. 'We always push much deeper than the other couples.'

She catches the pin and firmly shoves it into one of the holes before approaching the carcass with her skinning dagger in hand. 'It doesn't matter if we're the last ones out. We still provide our share.'

'No, it doesn't matter at all.' Yelqen dons his warm clothing. 'Oh, what a wonderful feeling.'

Isfael smiles at her husband as she begins decapitating the doe. 'I'll be done with this shortly.'

He readies the bota bag. 'Just let me know when you want to wash the blood off.'

The female elf carries the severed head over to the totem and pushes it onto one of the unmarked pegs, making sure that the rod goes into the hole at the base of the skull, before wrapping the tendons around the pillar and tying them off on the opposite side. 'There. That should hold until it rots off.' She gives the head a wiggle to make sure it will stay put. 'Yes, that's definitely not going anywhere. Unless Halfmoon comes by and rips it off again.'

Yelqen walks closer with the water bag. 'It was the elk head that fell off. We can come back next season and stalk those again. Or maybe boars.'

Isfael rinses her hands. 'I'd much rather hunt deer. I don't fancy going after an angry pig with a spear. But we must do as the tastes of the villagers command.'

'Would you even be able to come hunting with me next season? I don't think the old wytch will be seeing another winter through as the superior. She might decide to hand that honour over to you and be done with it.'

Isfael gives a slight shake of the head. 'The wytch superior has shown no interest in stepping down. She'll probably stay put until Nammu decides her time has come and calls her to the afterlife.'

Yelqen closes the spout of the bota bag with a softwood stopper. He walks back to his pack to put his gear away, leaving only his wife's warm clothes out. 'Hunting these forests won't be the same without you.'

'You, Arcim and his hunting partner can pool your efforts together. I'm sure he'll say yes to that.'

Yelqen hands his wife her trousers. 'We've already spoken about it and he's happy with that decision.'

Isfael begins donning her warm clothes. 'One step ahead of the rest, I see.'

'Well, you were bound to stop hunting at some stage. The child won't remain unnoticed for much longer.'

She smiles at her husband. 'I would've loved to come down here with both of you, teach our child to hunt and gut. Teach it the ways of life here in the forest.' Her expression turns a little sad. 'But the village needs a healer and it's as you said before: The wytch superior might not be around for much longer. Then again, she is a tough one.'

'That old leather slipper will be clinging to life until our hair goes grey.'

Isfael gives her husband a disapproving stare. 'Come now, was there any need for such disrespect?'

'Yes. She hates you. Everybody can see that she's jealous of you.'

'I don't think so.' Isfael waves the accusation off.

Yelqen takes up his end of the spear. 'You're too nice, wife of mine. You should be a little meaner to those around you.'

They hoist the carcass off the ground. 'There is enough heartache in the world as is. I do not wish to add to it.'

'That's what I love most about you. You are the purest of souls.'

'You know, you don't have to woo me anymore. We are married,' she quips light-heartedly.

'But I like wooing you.'

HARVEST CAMP

Walking down the wildlife path they've used so many times before, the couple chats about child names and future plans. The cold wind continues its relentless assault on the world as if it was willing the winter to arrive sooner. Scattered rain showers spit at the land, but they don't do enough to actually drench the soil.

Yelqen slows down a little. 'Something's approaching.'

He has barely spoken the words when two grey wolves appear around the bend, their dark yellow eyes fixed on the pair, their mouths open slightly as they pant.

Isfael holds her hand out and snaps her fingers. 'Aye, Nuki and Naki. You two coming to say hello?'

The two wolves break into a run, heading straight for the female elf and her companion. They run past, snarling as they go, before turning around and encircling the pair.

Both wolves try their luck with the carcass, but Yelqen can see their intentions. 'Nah! Down! Both of you!' The wolves obey, but their eyes never leave the fresh kill. 'Good pups. Return to Father.'

There is a reluctance in the wolves as they are torn between obeying and trying to get a bite.

'Go!' Yelqen barks at the animals and this time they listen.

Isfael watches them trot off. 'We should get ourselves a pup again. Perhaps two this time.'

'Yes, we should. Just so long as Nuki isn't the father of litter –

he's too stupid to be any good.'

She gives her husband a disapproving glance over the shoulder. 'That's not a very nice thing to say.'

'It might not be nice, but it is true. Naki on the other hand, he would father some really worthwhile cubs.'

'Or we can go into the forest, seek out a lone pup whose parents might have fallen foul of some other predator.'

Yelqen pulls a face to show his disapproval. 'I'd rather try and convince the chieftess to give us a pup out of her next litter. Those grassland-wolves are beautiful beasts, I like their less scruffy appearance. These forest wolves look a bit unkempt, don't they?'

'I like the wild aura of our forest beasts. I'd much rather have one of them.' A thought occurs to Isfael. 'What if we can convince the chieftess to mate her male with one of the other females in the village? She only ever allows her wolves to mate as a pair.'

Yelqen rolls his lower lip out. 'That could make for an interesting coupling. But I'll let you worry about convincing the chieftess, you have a much better rapport with her than I do.'

'I'm the village wytch, not the daughter of a ruler. I doubt I'd have much more sway than anyone else.'

'Well, I can marry you off to some old chief in a faraway land. That should gain you the clout you desire,' Yelqen replies and gives his wife a broad grin.

She smiles at the jest. 'My word, never knew I married such a visionary.'

They share a wry smile with each other while continuing down the narrow track, their conversation turning back to their unborn child.

The path peters out into a small clearing where they stop once more to greet the guardian of the north approach who has been sitting on the large wooden bench for almost half a day now, watching, waiting. When he sees the couple Huwen smiles and gets up, placing his recurve bow down on his seat and adjusting his belt to make sure that his overly long carp-tongue sword is hanging by his side and not between his legs; he is the only male in the Bravin Clan strong enough to wield the oversized blade.

They lay the deer carcass down and approaches the guard. Yelqen is the first to greet Huwen by clasping a hand behind the large male's head. 'Love you, Father. Good to see you again.'

Huwen returns the gesture, having to bend down slightly as he is a giant amongst the elves at six and half feet. 'Love you, Child.' He moves over to the female and repeats the greeting, seeing her as an adopted daughter. 'Love you, Child.'

Isfael can smell the sweet, scented oils in his hair. 'Love you, Father. Good to see you again.'

'Glad you're back and in one piece, both of you,' Huwen says as he steps back.

The two wolves come bounding out of the treeline and head straight for the dead animal on the ground, but their master is quick to stop them. 'Oi! Go bench, stay!'

Both wolves stop, their heads swivelling between their master and the carcass.

'I said bench.' Huwen's voice is more authoritative this time.

They finally obey and trot over to the seating area where they lay down next to the master's bag, their eyes never leaving the kill.

Huwen adjusts his pile-woven cloak, making sure the bronze clasp hasn't come undone. 'Well, I won't keep you, because you two must be starving.'

'See you at evening meal?' Isfael asks and picks up the spear.

'Unfortunately I must say no. I'm to do double duty.'

Yelqen gives him an incredulous look. 'Double guard duty? But why?'

'Inus, the moron, got his arm broken. He thought it would be funny to startle one of the horses while it was grazing.' Huwen rests his right hand on the pommel of his sword as he speaks. 'So now one of us has to work twice as much to ensure that all of the villagers can sleep soundly.'

Isfael takes up her end of the spear, frowning as she lifts it onto her shoulder. 'Why was I not summoned?'

The guard returns to the bench and sits down, making himself comfortable on the draped yak skin. 'We sorted the fool. Go, hand that thing over to the stewards, grab some food and get some rest.'

They wave goodbye to the guard and head towards the track that will lead them to the camp, their departure watched with anticipation by Nuki and Naki who continuously lick their lips.

'Calm down, you two.' Huwen reaches into his bag and gives each wolf a piece of dried meat. 'Here, have this instead, you greedy buggers.'

The perpetual dusk of the thick forest abruptly ends when they walk into the perimeter of the old village that has been repurposed as a Harvesting Camp. Generations of villagers who cleared the area have prevented trees from growing anywhere near the low palisade fence that surrounds the camp, only nettles and dandelions have managed to take root.

Entering through the northern gate, they make their way between the long-hut situated in the middle of the clearing and the horse stable that is roughly fifty paces away. The large semi-circle is buzzing with activity. Youngsters on the cusp of adulthood scurry back and forth between the open-air structure of the stewards' barn and the Luhup River that makes up the southern edge of the harvesting camp. They've been tasked with washing items and collecting up fresh water for use in the kitchen and prepping area, and they're closely followed by their younger siblings who can't look after themselves just yet.

The couple make their way over to the open barn where they lay their hunt down on the ancient, worn-out flagstones. Isfael unties the ropes and steps aside so that her husband can hoist the carcass up off the ground. She grabs a pair of sharpened stakes off a nearby table and shoves them through the deer's tarsal skins and into the holes of the butcher's rack.

Nearby one of the children stumbles over her own feet and falls onto the heavy leather bucket she was carrying, splitting the material and ruining the water container.

'I'm sorry, I'm sorry.' Her voice crackles with fear of being smacked for her clumsiness.

Her mother helps her up. 'It's fine. Take the broken skin to the leather workers and go fetch a replacement out of the store.'

'I didn't mean to break it.'

'I know, just go and do what you've been asked to do.' The female elf nods at the young wytch and her husband before returning to her task of meat preservation.

Four tame wolves approach the barn, drawn closer by the sweet smell of a fresh kill that has somehow wormed its way out of the thick stench generated by the vinegar and herbs used to prevent the meat from spoiling. Their owners are quick to retrieve the animals, either dragging them away by the scruff of their necks or forcing them to obey by slight hints of magic.

A stewardess by the name of Cathe places a large copper dish under the carcass into which she pours a small measure of water and trona powder so she can catch and kill any lingering ticks that decide to abandon their dead host.

Cathe is dressed in a dark linen skirt and tunic which compliments her silvery hair. 'Did you see worms, slugs or growths in any of the organs?'

'No, Mother, there were no signs of disease or parasites in this one,' Isfael answers while picking at the dried blood under her fingernails.

'The meat smells good. You've done well.' Cathe gives a slight nod as she pulls the chest cavity open to look inside, picking out a few leaves that fell in during the return trek. Satisfied with the catch she approaches her daughter and they touch foreheads. 'Love you, Child.'

Isfael places her hand behind her parent's head. 'Love you, Mother.'

Cathe does the same with her quasi-adopted son. 'Love you, Child.'

'Love you, Mother.'

Cathe turns to her daughter again and presses the palm of her hand on the lower abdomen. 'How is my grandchild?'

Isfael pulls a face. 'Mother, please. It'll be another year before my bump really begins to show.'

'And I want my grandchild to hear my voice as often as possible. Want him or her to know who the spoiler is.'

'No, you're not spoiling the child. I forbid it.' Yelqen's tone is stern yet playful.

Cathe slaps him on the upper arm. 'Yes, I am spoiling the child! It is my right as the grandmother. Now go and get yourselves cleaned up for the evening meal, we'll bring it over in a bit.'

Yelqen rubs the spot where he just got smacked and lays the drama on thick for a laugh. 'Ah, ah. The old stewardess has harmed me. My arm has been undone and I'll never raise my spear again.'

Cathe gives him a couple of playful blows. 'Get out of here before I really lay one on you, silly child. Go.'

Isfael smiles; she enjoys watching her mother and her husband have these playful moments. 'I must go and see Inus. I hear tell he got kicked by one of the cart animals.'

'Indeed he did. It is beyond our understanding why he thought it would be a good idea to slap the hindquarters of a horse when it is grazing. Luckily they were in the western field, close enough to hear his screams.'

'Where is he now?'

Cathe gives a shrug. 'Somewhere in camp.'

Yelqen holds a hand out to his wife. 'Give me that headless arrow. I'll go and ask Deima to re-tip it for you.'

She surrenders the requested item and heads up the gentle slope towards the main fire pit where most of the other hunting couples are sitting and chatting.

It is midday and all of the sixty short-term inhabitants appear to be busy with something. Children under the tutelage of their parents learn their trade while youngsters and young adults who are already versed in their work go at it with breakneck speed; they graft at a relentless pace for fear of getting smacked and because free time awaits once the day's quotas are filled.

Among those who work the hardest are the tanners who are trying to get all the raw hides ready for preservation or further refinement to meet the needs of the village. Deer skins that have been soaking in ash water for the last two weeks are scraped clean before they are loaded onto a wagon.

An old male elf stops his four grandchildren from piling any more of the skins on the wagon; he can tell that the limits of the horse's capabilities are close to being reached. With a gentle tug on the reins, he gets the animal moving and leads it towards the gate in the southwestern corner of the camp. The children fall in behind the cart and follow it.

Another cart enters through the same gate, its axle creaking under the weight of the hides that have been marinating in the peat since the last harvesting season. The young female and her two brothers realise their mistake too late and get behind the cart to help the horse get up the slope. They scream at each other and curse the lay of the land but get no further.

Alerted by the noise their father runs out of the leather working hut to see what the commotion is all about. He is quick to go to their aid and help get the cart onto level ground where it is secured to stop it rolling back. Despite the youngsters' apologies Menim smacks each one of them behind the head, punishing them for ignoring his teachings. They are ordered to get over the discomfort and unload the bog-tanned hides.

None of the elves who have witnesses the scene pays the harsh discipline any heed; they see it as part of daily life.

Young adults working with the camp stewards load the prepared meat into a small hand-drawn cart which they roll out of the camp, heading for the same peat bog where the hides are preserved. There they will wrap the precious commodity in velum before burying it in the water-logged soil for preservation, leaving the hunks of flesh to marinate until next year.

Scavenger parties enter the camp, the leather bags draped

over their shoulders are full to the brim with edible plants. All of them converge on the stewards' barn where they unload their finds. River water is used to wash the soil off the root vegetables before they are stored in wooden crates filled with damp sand.

A male hunter by the name of Arcim runs over and playfully shoulder-barges his friend. 'Yelqen, you dried up old lentil. I see you finally got back to camp, a day late and a deer short.'

'As if you had dropped off more than one carcass.' He smiles at the other male. 'How are you?'

Arcim lets out a short whistle to call his companion. 'Chub! Come!' He waits for the wolf to get close before answering Yelqen's question. 'I'm doing great. Actually managed to bag two deer. First one was a normal hunt. Second one was pure luck. I was out looking for mushrooms, at the behest of one of the cooks, when I sneezed and startled a young buck who was grazing nearby. Poor thing ran headfirst into a tree and broke its neck.'

'I can sense the lies pouring out your mouth and straight into my ears,' Yelqen remarks on the exploits of the other male, but it is done in good humour. 'You most probably found a dead one while you were out scavenging for your mind-melting plants, shoed the flies away and dragged the rotten carcass back here.'

Arcim gives his pal a playful shove. 'Shhh... dammit. I don't want others to know I dabble in the darker side of mushroom consumption.'

Yelqen pats Chub's head as the wolf bumps into him. 'Calm down, you're hardly the only person in our clan who dries and eats that stuff.'

'I just enjoy the feeling of freedom they give me. Nothing better than floating through the world on a layer of bliss.'

Yelqen smiles. 'You don't get a glimpse at Nammu's soul while you are drifting around in your clouds of pure enjoyment?'

Arcim lets out a snort to show his disinterest. 'Nah, I'm too blunt to sense anything past my real-world body. Wasn't born with the gift of feeling, unlike you and your wife.'

'That's just the way life has cast us,' Yelqen replies before he points in the direction of the large tent on the bank of the river. 'You coming along for a stroll and a chat? I need to drop this headless arrow off for repairs.'

Arcim waves the invite off. 'No, sorry. I was actually on my way back up to the old long-hut to get my bow. I want Fauk to have a look at it. I think the upper limb is beginning to separate. See you by the fire pit once you've completed your errand?'

Yelqen nods and continues down towards the large tent.

Isfael offers a greeting to everyone seated by the fire in front of the long-hut and removes her heavy tool belt before sitting down on the log bench by the door. The hunters, who bid the young wytch welcome, are in good spirits; they all have a tale to share about a close encounter with some untamed wolves or bears of both walks. One of the couples are regaling the group with their near misadventure, using a pantomime to describe how they had to run for their lives when confronted by the biggest Co'atal-bear they had ever seen. Everyone enjoys the exaggerated descriptions of the infamous two-legged beast known as Halfmoon because of the distinctive scar on its left pectoral.

Laughter envelops them while they continue to dress their daggers; with stone hammers and anvils they beat the edges of the bronze blades into the desired thickness, followed up by the use of whetstones to refine the bevels and sharpen the knives.

Inus plops himself down on the log, right next to the healer who addresses him.

'Greetings. I was told that you suffered a mishap. Let me have a look at it.'

Inus' manners are short. 'Too late, mushroom brewer, my arm is mending.'

Isfael ignores the belittlement of her abilities. 'No, it is not. I can see by the shade of your skin that you're not in a good way. Now stop being such a wet shoe and give me that arm.'

'Just hold out your paw, Inus, and let the wytch have a look,' one of the hunters, Ghun, orders.

Reluctantly the young male stretches out his arm and grimaces with pain.

Isfael thanks him and begins her chant so that she may imbue herself with magic. 'Mother Nammu, loving Mother, grant me the healer sight so that I may see what lies beneath.' Her eyes emit a dull red glow, allowing her vision to pierce his flesh. 'Your bones... are not aligned, Inus. I have to reset them if you wish to regain full use of this hand.'

He tries to pull away. 'No, my arm is fine.'

She refuses to let go of his limb, her glowing eyes locked onto his. It is an unsettling sight for the young adult. 'Listen here, horse teaser, if you do not let me set these bones, your muscles will shrink and you'll be in pain for the rest of your life. Is that what you want? To be a burden on the clan? Forever suffering and unable to contribute?'

Inus yanks his arm out of her grasp and cradles it against his chest. 'Alright, I'll let you work your healing touch on me, but I need something for the pain.'

Isfael uses a simple chant to break the spell. 'Thank you, Mother, for this gift. Make normal again my flesh.' She blinks a few times and her eyes return to their usual light brown. 'I'll go into my stash of medicine plants and prepare a potion. In the meantime, you get comfortable on your sleeping pile.'

Inus stands up and walks towards the long-hut; he is clearly unstable on his feet. Seeing him sway spurs two nearby males to aid their injured fellow.

Yelqen nears his wife and sits down beside her. 'Couldn't help but overhear that. Do you need help with anything?'

Isfael hands her tool belt over and gets to her feet. 'No, it's nothing too serious. Do you mind finishing up my blades while I tend to this issue?'

Yelqen takes the belt. 'Not at all. Before you go, I've given your arrow to Deima. He says he'll have it fixed by tomorrow. Now, go and see to the one who slaps the arses of grazing horses.'

The last comment draws a few giggles out of the other

hunters. Close by, Arcim is tilling his bow while the master bowyer watches the limbs of the weapon to see how they curve; Fauk's expression betrays the fact that there is indeed something wrong with it.

Three male elves kneel down beside the bed of their injured fellow. Two of them have been tasked with holding the patient still while Menim, the leather worker, has to secure the splints in place; he was chosen because of his accuracy and skills with knots.

Nakka presses down on the shoulders, using his left leg to pin the uninjured arm. 'Ready, Wytch.'

Harlon straddles the legs to keep them secure. 'Ready, Wytch.'

Isfael closes her eyes and begins her ancient polyphonic chant. When she opens them again, they are glowing like before, only this time the light appears more intense because she is sitting in the dimly lit interior of the long-hut. She shoves a bit of rolled-up hard leather in her patient's mouth. 'Here, bite down on this.'

Fear has contorted Inus' face, but he obliges.

The young wytch places one foot under the armpit of her ward while taking hold of his wrist and elbow. 'You must relax your muscles. The more you fight me, the longer this will take. So relax, relax.'

Unable to do as instructed, Inus nods but keeps his fist clenched.

Isfael asks him to relax one more time, but again he fails to do so. 'You're such a typical youngster male. Big mouth when everything is working, but utterly useless when you have the slightest ouchy.'

The elf frowns at the belittlement. He is about to mumble something in protest but is cut short when the wytch pulls on his wrist with all her might. Spittle and muffled screams make their way past the leather bit in his mouth.

Isfael checks the alignment of the bones. 'Now, get the planks on.'

Menim makes quick work of setting the splints in place and tying them down. 'Done.'

Isfael checks the bones again, her head bobbing up and down and from side to side to see past the obstructing splints. 'Good, that will keep...'

She is interrupted by Nakka, the male who is holding Inus' shoulders down. 'Look, he's passed out – his face has gone the colour of tallow and his eyes have rolled back in his head.'

Isfael places the arm down and looks at Inus' chest. 'Dammit, his heart has stopped. Step away, I need to get it beating again.'

The helpers let go and move back, they seem confused by the healer's words.

Isfael flicks the leather bit out of her patient's mouth and recites a new chant; it is one that she's only just started experimenting with and she isn't too sure how much of her life it will drain. 'Mother Nammu, grant me the power to punch through.' Placing her psalm on Inus' chest, she takes a deep breath and hits him with a blast of kinetic energy that sends dust particles flying off his tunic in all directions. Isfael tries to check his heart, but her healer sight is failing. 'Dammit, I need to work on this.' She digs deeper into her soul and draws up another bout of energy to hit the unconscious male. Its force makes his whole body convulse.

The glow in Isfael's eyes goes out and she slumps to the floor, limp and lacking colour in her face. Inus on the other hand gasps for air and begins to cough. Harlon is quick to flip the injured male on his side before bolting out the door of the long-hut, his mind set on finding Yelqen.

Together Menim and Nakka lift the semi-conscious healer up and carry her over to her pile of sleeping skins where they lay her down.

'Did you see that? Did you see what she did?'

'Of course I saw, I was standing right next to you...'

NEW MAGIC

S lowly Isfael's consciousness returns and she opens first one eye, then the other. Her head is pounding and her limbs feel heavy. Sitting up is normally a simple enough movement, but a lack of strength makes it extremely difficult.

'Thank Mother Nammu, you're awake. You were lying so still that your heart barely made a sound. I thought you had gone into the afterlife.' Yelqen is knelt down beside his wife, steadying her.

'Give me... a moment. I need to see if the child is still alive.' She gets into a squatting position and presses her fingers against her vulva, trying to feel for any abnormalities. She holds her hand up to look at it. 'Good, no blood. I can also feel my heartbeat down there, all good signs that the child is still alive and drawing strength from me.'

Yelqen holds a bowl out to her as she sits back down. 'Here, eat. Regain your strength.' He sits down across from her. 'What happened?'

Ravaged by hunger, she lifts the bowl up to her mouth and slurps some of the food down, not caring for etiquette. Trapped air rolls out of her throat. 'Hoo, my. Apologies for that. I should really eat a bit more slowly.'

'Isfael, what happened the other day? Menim, Nakka and Harlon are talking about you hitting Inus with some kind of wind, or power. They believe it is some sort of magic they have never seen before.'

19

The young wytch finishes the stew and places the bowl down. 'Damn. I've not known hunger like that since I learned to use my healer sight.'

'Isfael, are you going to explain this to me or not?'

She nods and points at the door. 'Any souls close by?'

Yelqen reaches out with his magic sense. 'Not close enough to hear us speak.'

She moves up to her husband and explains: 'I've been thinking about the clan, about the fact that so many of the villagers struggle with heart problems. The original Bravins, that is. I've spoken to a few of the wytches in Keties and they do not deal with nearly as many troubled hearts as I do. Few of them have acquaintances in Kelpie and Tin and even they've not heard of so many heart problems. This year alone we've already lost four people to the curse, among them Limma's brother, a strong male. Drops dead in the middle of the village, nothing I could do for him. That's why I've been working on this new technique. Maybe I can keep the people alive long enough to figure out why they have these problems.'

'How did you come up with a way of hitting someone without moving your hands? That is the part that has our fellows pooing their trousers. They say they could feel some sort of power emanating off you.' Yelqen's voice is quivering slightly.

'I began my new training regime shortly after Limma's brother was buried.'

Yelqen interrupts her. 'How did this talent come about?'

'Well, my love, if you let me speak then I'll explain it to you.' Isfael gets onto her knees, her face lit up with excitement, her voice low. 'I used a piece of aged meat, dosed with aconite to kill the cat that stalks the medicine hut.'

'Wh... what?' Yelqen is aghast. 'Why would you be so cruel?'

Isfael holds her finger up to her mouth. 'I did it to better understand the workings of the heart.'

'We all know how the heart works. The head tells it to thump like a drum.'

'That's the easy explanation. But why do so many Bravins die of heart failure?' She takes her husband's hand in hers. 'I used the cat's death to learn about substances that flow through our veins. I knew what I was looking for and I could see it, see the aconite in its blood. If I can figure out what is causing the heart problems, I'll know what to look for, what to draw out with my healer's touch. The cat showed me one thing I can work with, because I killed it on purpose and in reviving it, I managed to learn another technique that has proved itself useful.'

Yelqen shakes his head. 'That is a cruel thing to do to a helpless cat.'

Isfael huffs the remark. 'The cat is fine. It was miserable for a few days, but it quickly recovered. By day it sleeps in the medicine hut, and at night it stalks around the food stores in search of vermin. I'm glad it allowed me to improve my understanding of how our bodies work.'

'Cats and elves are slightly different, wouldn't you say?'

'In shape, size and movement, yes... but we do have similar organs.' She picks up the bowl and gets to her feet. 'I need to take a dip in the wash pond and clean off the grime that I accumulated on the hunt yesterday. After that I wish to go to the small meadow and harvest some medicine plants.'

Yelqen gathers up the two wash bags, one with their dirty clothes in it and one containing the soaps they'll be using to wash themselves. 'I'll join you for that dip, I've not scrubbed myself since Naka told me that you had passed out. It's high time I rid my skin of this sweaty crust.'

Air wafting out of Isfael tunic makes her curious. 'I smell really bad, how long was I unconscious?'

'Almost three days.'

The reply drains the colour from her face. 'I should really be careful with that magic.'

'Hmmm, you really should,' Yelqen replies while pointing at her lower abdomen.

Isfael rolls her eyes while letting out an exasperated wail of annoyance.

People stop what they are doing as soon as they see the wytch exiting the long-hut. Isfael feels an uncomfortable atmosphere filling the camp and notices murmurs coming from all corners; everyone appears to be on edge. Not only can she sense the eyes on her, but she is also painfully aware of the unease in her husband who is much more sensitive to other people's auras and emotions.

'Ignore them. They'll soon forget what they've heard and come asking me for aid again.'

Yelqen shakes his head. 'It would seem that they're just uncertain of your abilities. You've done something that they've never heard of. It's not every day that a dead person is brought back from the afterlife.'

'Inus was not dead.' Isfael has to think fast to make her argument more meaningful. 'He was just lingering in a dusk-like place between this world and the next.'

'You say that as if you have some proof of that... dusk-like world.'

She gives a slight shrug of indifference. 'I could see the light in his brain. Acting fast kept that little fire burning, allowing his heart to spread its warmth throughout his body.' She waves her hand around. 'I think the people are unsure of me because I've displayed another magic talent. Now they're afraid that I'll become overburdened by all the spells, go insane and just start killing people for no reason.'

Yelqen raises his eyebrows at his wife. 'No, I don't think they are scared of you losing control, they are confused and uncertain about the female who snatched a soul out of the mouths of Cariion's wolf pack.'

'I'll just keep to myself until they need me again. Ease them into the comfort that I'm not mad with power.'

Yelqen has a crooked smile on his lips. 'Well, that might take a few years then, because you still have to contend with the wytch superior who refuses to relinquish her post.'

Isfael shakes her head. 'We'll leave such decisions up to time and the chief. For now I'm in dire need of a wash.'

Squeals of delight cut through the frigid air as the children enjoy the freedom that bathing offers them. Their playfulness, however, stops abruptly when the wytch rounds the low hedges that grow around the pond; they too have heard the murmurs and are scared of the healer's new abilities. Quickly, quietly they finish their bathing and leave, most of them scurrying away whilst covering their nudity with the simple linen cloths they would normally use for drying themselves.

'I hope this won't become a permanent thing.' Isfael's tone is almost defeatist. 'I don't want my child to be an outcast because of what the mother can do.'

'You said it yourself, only time can sort this thing out,' Yelqen says while dropping a piece of old leather on the muddy ground.

'Indeed.' The young wytch begins to undress, laying her clothes on the piece of square leather.

Another huntress rounds the low hedge and barks a question at the healer. 'Is it true?'

'Hello Limma. Is what true?' Isfael knows full well what her friend is asking about but decides to humour her.

'Ah, yes. Good morning. Apologies for my rudeness.' Limma gestures over her shoulder at the rest of the camp before she continues. 'So, is it true? Did you revive Inus after he had gone into the afterlife, by making his tired heart beat again?'

'It is, but his heart wasn't tired. It just stopped for a very short while.'

Limma lets out a little squeal of delight. 'Really? Do you think you could do it again?'

Isfael's eyes grow large with surprise. 'Uhm... yes, but don't set your expectations too high. I've only just learned this skill – I guess that's why most of the villagers are afraid of me now.'

'Pish posh. I've been living with fear most of my life. My family is rife with the Bravin curse. You do realise that you're the first wytch to cure death.' Limma's face is alive with hope.

Isfael smirks at the comment. 'I hardly cured death.' She

stares at her friend. 'Thank you for seeing past the other people's superstitions and coming to talk with me.'

'You are most welcome.' Limma takes her clothes off and lays them on the low hedgerow. 'I need a wash too. Been out digging for roots and worked up a sweat.'

Yelqen spares the other naked female no glances, instead he is staring lustfully at his wife while beating the suds out of their clothes with a wash-bat. The two females take turns washing each other's backs while chatting about trivial things while Yelqen sings to himself as he washes their clothes.

Isfael and Yelqen drape the last of her wet clothes over the drying frames that have been erected around the hearth in the long-hut. They dry their hair as best they can before getting dressed; she dons her favourite attire consisting of a long thick skirt and a double-layer tunic, while her husband puts on his trousers and long-sleeved shirt before draping a thin woollen cloak over his shoulders.

Yelqen picks up the leather bag he carries with him wherever he goes and checks the contents. 'There's two winter cloaks should it rain or perhaps snow, but I think it's still too warm for the latter. And water, food and all of the dressing stones we'll need to make our knives nice and sharp. All set to go.'

The young wytch puts her tool belt on and touches each of the bronze implements, reciting their names. 'Mattock. Axe. Skinning dagger. Fighting dagger...' She drapes a large leather pouch over her shoulder. '... and the collection bag. I'm all set to go, too.'

Limma is nearby, having just gotten dressed herself. 'We off then?'

'You want to join me on my medicine harvest?' Isfael is slightly taken back by her friend's question.

'Indeed I do.'

She glares at Limma while slinging her quiver over her shoulder and retrieving her bow. 'You've never joined me on one of these scavenges before.'

'You've never upset the whole village before, and a friend does not leave a friend in the lurch. So come, young wytch, let's go for a relaxing walk among the trees of this land.'

Limma appears to be very perked up, which makes Yelqen smile. 'An extra pair of eyes to look for danger is never a bad thing.'

Isfael shrugs. 'I'm not complaining, let's go.'

They exit the long-hut and set off for the clearing they call the Glen. Yelqen, who is carrying his hunting spear over the shoulder, leads the way out of camp through the east gate. Birdsong and the constant hustle of the wind accompany the small party as they move along the old deer track while Limma engages the healer in a conversation about the physical working of the heart.

Halfway to the destination Yelqen stops to gather himself; he is clearly upset, his breathing erratic and his face pale.

'Do you want to head back, my love?' The concern in Isfael's voice is evident.

'N-no, no,' Yelqen stammers. 'I... I'll be fine. Just need to get a grip of myself.'

'Why are you so on edge?' Limma enquires while checking their surroundings, fighting dagger in her hand, ready for action.

'We're heading... we're heading to the meadow where I found my mother two years back,' Yelqen manages, sounding out of breath.

Limma grimaces. 'Apologies, I completely forgot about that.'

'No need to apologise. You can't keep track of everything that everyone has to deal with.'

'Are you angered by that day?' Limma asks out of curiosity.

'No. That was a hard year. The wolves were starving, just like we were. My mother should not have ventured into the forest alone.' He tries to sound indifferent, but the hurt still shows through.

'At least you have something to channel your feelings. I lost most of my family to some stupid curse. Where do I redirect my anger? Which low individual laid that damn curse on us Bravin originals?' Limma raises the weapon to have a better look at the blade. 'So many dead and no one knows why.'

Isfael lets out a soft sigh; she finds it hard to deal with all the raw emotions that are surrounding her right now. She steels herself by accepting that she can do very little to ease her husband's troublesome memories, but she can at least endeavour to eliminate curse that has ravaged Bravin for generations.

'Sorry,' Limma mumbles as she watches the bronze metal give off its characteristic amber sheen in the dim light of the day, 'I should not dwell on that which has passed.'

Yelqen gathers himself. 'And I must accept that my mother is no longer here and move on. I too should stop dwelling on past events.'

As he begins walking he chants to himself so that he may awaken his magic gift. After a few moments, however, Yelqen stops again and lowers his spear. 'Weapons ready. There's something close by, something... big... and angry.'

Limma immediately gets into a fighting stance and utters a quick chant so that she can search for the warmth given off by the animals of the forest. Her eyes emit a slight yellow glow. 'I don't see anything bigger than a hare.'

Isfael whips her bow off her back and slots an arrow into place.

'I see... a pack blaiffs over there.' Limma gives an indication with her free hand. 'But they seem to be going away.'

'Sensed them before I sensed the raw power. Those two-legged wolves are running scared, running away... but from what?' Yelqen pivots on the spot, the tip of his weapon indicating where the sense is coming from 'Shit. Shit. It's a Co'atal-bear. It's hungry, far too hungry to be going to sleep for the winter.'

Limma catches a glimpse of the large warm spot moving through the trees. 'Shit is the right word... that is Halfmoon. He stole Prenya's and Furnar's kill a few days back.'

Isfael begins to back away. 'The plants can wait till later – we need to leave now.'

'No, we don't,' Yelqen responds. 'You go and harvest the medicines, and I'll stay here and keep that bear under eye.'

'Don't be an idiot, you stand no chance against that thing.'

'I'll stay here with him,' Limma offers. She has her eyes fixed on the animal as she swaps her dagger for her axe.

'Both of you need to…'

'Just go and get the damn medicines. Make it quick,' Yelqen hisses at his wife. 'The clan needs them.'

Isfael hits back at her husband. 'You'll apologise to me later for taking that tone.'

'Yes, yes. Now go, hurry.'

The wytch holsters the arrow and slings her bow over her shoulder as she backs away, keeping herself low to the ground. Her companions follow suit; for now they are lucky because the wind is blowing in their favour.

Halfmoon, who picks at the bark of a tree, his nose constantly searching for something to eat, is oblivious to the three elves that are only a few hundred paces away. A fallen tree draws his attention and, upon closer inspection, he discovers several clusters of wood-eating grubs that have made themselves comfortable for the winter. Using his immense strength and ape-like front paws, the two-legged bear rips the hardwood trunk apart so that he can get to his treat. It's not nearly enough to fatten him up, but it will do until he can find something more substantial.

MILE-MARKER

I t is still dark when the camp stewards and the night watch go around the various tents to wake the sleeping youngsters. One of the guards enters the long-hut and begins rousing his fellow villagers. Some of them quietly express their disapproval while others get up with little in the way of complaining.

One of the males closest to the hearth shuffles over to it and begins stoking the fire by laying thin strips of wood and dried bark on the glowing embers. Long matches, made of rush plant material soaked in animal fat, are used to light the candles, each flame sputtering into existence as the tallow begins to burn. Polished copper candelabras with concave back plates stop the flames licking up the walls whilst also scattering the light throughout the building.

The events of the last few days have made most of the clan uneasy around the young wytch, and they give her a fairly wide berth whenever she appears. Isfael tries to look indifferent to their behaviour, but deep down she feels insulted and belittled. She was handed an incredible talent at birth and, since discovering her powers as a youngster, she's been striving to improve her skills and use them for the benefit of others. Now she is facing an uphill struggle thanks to the ignorant beliefs of their forebears that are loosely based on a legend.

Yelqen can sense the hurt in his wife and hugs her. 'Don't let them grind you down. One day, when their health fails them, they'll come crawling to you for aid.'

'I know, but I don't want them to seek me out of desperation, I want them to trust me. Why is my talent such a problem for them? I saved someone's life and yet they treat me like I have brothel rot.' Isfael shrugs the embrace off so that she may continue to tidy up her sleeping skins.

For the briefest of moments Yelqen contemplates the outcome of slicing someone open with his dagger so that they are forced to ask his wife for help, but he restrains himself, realising that such actions will be foolish and would cause even more dissent amongst the folks of Bravin.

Lighting the way with torches everyone heads down to the wash pond to rid themselves of their slumber. Yelqen walks down with the others, fills a bucket with water and then carries it back up to the long-hut where his wife is waiting for him; she has decided it is best to keep a distance from the villagers for now.

Large clay pots full of stew are set out by the cooks, allowing everyone to have a hearty breakfast before they start the day. Limma and Arcim are the only elves who sit with the semi-outcast couple.

With their stomachs full, the Bravin clan get to work breaking down their camp and getting everything ready for loading. Carts laden with trade goods are lined up on the side of the track that leads north while the empty ones are directed to where they are needed. It only takes the villagers an hour to pack up.

Nailing the long-hut's door shut is always the last thing they do before they leave.

Huwen approaches the old Master Bowyer and hands him the stone hammer. 'Here you go. Oldest male always gets the honour.'

Fauk takes the tool and gives him a wry smile. 'Don't be so smug, young billy goat, one day you'll be the one wielding this thing.'

'I'm only four years your junior. Chances are we'll both go

down to feed the worms at the same time.'

'I doubt that. Ragweed like you seems to cling on much longer than it should.' Fauk's sarcastic remark makes everyone grin with amusement, everyone except Inus who is moping around and cradling his arm.

Klouven is hard at work organising the order in which the caravan will move. All of the food carrying carts are ushered to the front so that they are free to carry on should the much heavier trade wagons get stuck in the soft soil. Leading the way, as always, will be the steward's cart; it is mostly empty, allowing the cooks and the night watch to catch up on some much-needed rest. Inus is the only other individual who is allowed to join the sleepers because of his brush with death and the powerful pain relief tea that the wytch brewed for him.

Ghun notices the caravan master stop next to one of the carts grasping at his chest. 'Klouven, are you feeling unwell?'

'No. Mind the carts, not me. Go away, do as you're told.' He waves the other male off, but each word is accompanied by a slight gasp for air.

The old hunter picks up on Klouven's troubled breathing, but he decides not to act on it as he knows that there is not much he can do or say to convince the caravan master to relinquish his position and stay with the wytches who could help him if needed. Instead Ghun makes his way down the line, checking each horse to ensure it has been hitched correctly.

Navigating under a moonless sky will be difficult. The risk of a wheel slipping into the waterlogged mud on either side of the narrow tracks is a constant worry for everyone, but the clan has come up with a solution: Youngsters carrying torches are sent up ahead so they can point out where the compacted soil ends and the problem areas begin.

Klouven walks down the line, talking to himself while double-checking every horse and cart, much to the dismay of the animal-husbands who have just been through the same routine with Ghun. Satisfied that everything is up to his standard, Klouven eventually cracks his whip as a signal for them to start moving. The animals are coaxed forward by their handlers who are careful not to stress them.

Slowly but surely the horizon grows brighter, paying testament to the coming dawn. The first rays of light break over the curve of the world, bathing everything in gold. Resident birds perched amongst the autumn leaves chirp and warble their songs of joy and lament, their calls made visible by the water vapour in their breath.

Large flocks of migratory fowl can be seen in the sky, their formations directed south to warmer lands beyond the horizon where they can escape the harsh touch of the encroaching winter. Everyone in the caravan remains vigilant as there is no telling which sort of dangers might be lurking amongst the dense trees.

The sun is still low in the sky when the harvesters enter a large clearing littered with rocks and moss-covered boulders. In the middle, where the three tracks meet, the caravan must split up into its two columns. One will continue north, up the ever-increasing gradient towards the village in the clouds, while the other will make its way west.

A lone copper beech stands in the heart of the triangle, its enormous purple canopy at odds with the other giants of the forest, for most of them are quickly donning their seasonal ambers, reds and yellows. Scattered throughout the uniform change are the evergreen firs whose colours are much less striking than the foliage of the mile-marker tree.

Males bid their families farewell, promising to return once the riches have been gathered.

Isfael tries to force a smile to show strength, but her expression is lopsided because of the tears she is fighting back; unable to suppress them any longer, she presses her forehead tightly against that of her husband. 'I'll miss you.'

'It won't be long before we see each other again. Two weeks at most and I'll be with you again, just be patient.'

She places both hands behind his head and touches his nose with hers, a sign of desperation in the elven cultures. 'I'll hold you to that.'

Yelqen places his hand on her cheek. 'You always do and I always deliver.'

He tries to leave but she wraps her arms around his chest and kisses him on the mouth before resting her face against his clavicle. Those standing nearby are appalled by the show of affection; such extreme acts of intimacy are best left for the marriage chamber.

It is with great reluctance that Isfael takes a step back. 'We'll be waiting for you.'

Yelqen kneels down and kisses her stomach. 'Take care of your mother, little one.'

Klouven cracks his whip and calls: 'Time to go and do some trade!' Dissatisfied by the pace of the horses he cracks the whip again. 'Heyaa! Move! Pick it up!'

The last few goodbyes are said and the two columns move off in their respective directions. They soon lose sight of each other.

LECCY BRIDGE

It is mid-morning when the trade column of the Bravin caravan rolls past the village's graveyard; all except Klouven wave at the sculpted stones that function as grave markers. They shout their greetings to let the dead know that they've not been forgotten. Up ahead they can see the edge of the Co'atal Forest where a sudden decrease in tree density and two large rocks either side of the track mark the end of their territory. On one of the rectangular blocks is a crest that represents the Bravin clan and their labours. The previous chief ordered the stonecutters to carve the representation of an oxhide ingot into the rock face and to flank the ingot with two knapped arrowheads, all of it underlined by a recurve bow and a bronze tipped spear. Not wanting to be outdone, the Keties clan chose to illustrate the might of their village's farming and trading abilities by having a sickle and balancing scales carved into the dark grey surface of the other stone.

The carts are halted and all of the males walk back to the last one where they stow their spears under the thick linen tarp and pull their swords a little further round their hips to hide the weapons under their cloaks.

Klouven starts to complain about the logistics and politics that accompany their actions. 'This shouldn't be necessary. If we wanted to make trouble, we would come at night when we're not seen. We wouldn't be stupid enough to walk around with our spears and swords out, waving them around like morons and

33

telling everyone that we are here to make war. We'd be sneaky about it. You don't start a fight by telling the other one that you want to hit him. If anything we should be holding our spears up so the guards can see what we have.'

The other males nod along to the Caravan Master's rant; it's become a tradition for them to listen to the same lament each year.

Arcim struggles to keep his composure and turns away. 'Dear Nammu, give me strength.'

'Be nice now,' Yelqen mumbles to his companion as he overhears the prayer directed at Mother Earth.

Klouven is still raging when he cracks his whip to get the horses moving again. 'Ridiculous laws! We're not the enemy here!'

Arcim rolls his eyes. 'This is the longest he's ever gone. When will he run out of breath?'

'You're right.' Yelqen suddenly realises the significance of his friends' observation. 'It just goes on and on.'

Klouven spins around to check his charges. 'Get back to your own cart, Arcim!'

He is totally taken aback by the order. 'Whoa! Calm yourself. I'm going... I'm going.'

'It's because of undisciplined pigs like you that we've to have all these rules!'

Yelqen's eyes grow large with shock. 'What!? Come now, that insult was not necessary.'

'You.' Klouven walks up to the younger male, his demeanour suggesting that he is ready for a fight. 'You have no morals. You and that wytch of yours. Kissing out in the open like that. Letting her practice unknown magic on the dead.'

The remark about his wife sets Yelqen's hackles on end. 'You had better shut up right now or I will hit you and I won't stop until I have a tooth or three as a trophy.'

'Enough! Both of you,' Ghun commands and shoves each of his fellows back. 'Klouven, get to your post. Yelqen, back to your cart.'

The caravan master points at the other male to appear intimidating before he moves back up to the front of the column.

'What's the matter with him? Is there a fungus growing on his head?' Yelqen asks while taking a moment to calm down.

'I will concede that he gets worse every year. I'll speak to the chief about his post. Perhaps someone else can take up the reins.' Ghun pats the elf on the back. 'Come, Yelqen, one last trip under the whip of the old goat.'

'Apologies, I didn't mean to get so angry at him, but he just really pushed the boat out when he made those remarks about Isfael.'

'He's been through a lot in life, allow him his bitterness.'

Yelqen doesn't agree with the last statement, but he's not one for pressing a point or an argument unless it is truly necessary. 'My anger will subside in a moment or two.'

'Good lad. Now we must hurry before we get shouted at again.'

They set off at a jogging pace to catch up with the column.

Mounds of smouldering earth fill the air with wood smoke, attended by the charcoal burners who watch their temporary kilns like hawks to make sure the wood isn't catching fire. They spare the passing traders a wave and a hello but not much else. Further along, the coppicing crews are hard at work collecting up the water-shoots that have sprouted from the stunted oaks trees, while others are busy training some of the new growth by bending the branches at the desired angles and tying them down; these will be left to harden so that they may be harvested in a few years and used as pick, axe or mattock handles.

Braiders move along the tree lines, using their copper sickles to harvest the nettles that grow there; the fiery plants will be spun into cord and twine by the hardened hands that are collecting them. Only a few of the workers stop what they are doing so that they may wave at their fellow elves who live atop the mountain that looms over the land.

It is almost midday when the caravan draws near to the first guard post of Keties, beyond which lays a long narrow wooden bridge, spanning the west branch of the Liyko River. Locals and traders moving between the bridgehead and the river harbour clog the causeway, forcing all other movers to stop.

Klouven calls his retinue to a halt and sits down on a marker stone beside the road, his mood still sour and his appearance bleak.

Members of the Keties Militia patrol the harbour to make sure that the traders adhere to the strict protocols of the slips; they carry round wooden shields in one hand and bronze tipped spears in the other. Hanging by their hips are carp-tongue swords, a design favoured by the elves. Each sword gleams in the dull autumn sun, proof that the members of the militia have taken the time to dress and sharpen their weapons, one of the many routines that speak volumes of their discipline.

Two of the soldiers approach the Bravin caravan and slowly walk around each cart, yet none of the mountain elves react to the authority flexing. Instead they continue to chat amongst themselves. Large wagons drawn by dual horse teams roll up behind the Bravin column; these are locals who have been working the narrow stretch of forest between the base of the grand peak and the river since early morning; for them it was a long day and the time to head home has finally come, the only problem is that they have to wait for the harbour to clear.

Boat captains and their business partners roar orders and obscenities at those under their employment, unashamed insults that are meant to spur their meagrely paid workers on. Truth of the matter is that they are pressed by the changing season, for once the snows begin to fall they'll lose access to the tributaries that feed the larger rivers.

Figures dressed in bright mustard-yellow and cherry-red liveries move between the piles of goods on the dockside; they are officers of the Keties Trader Collection. Their bright attire makes them stand out amongst the earth-coloured clothes of the workers.

Goblins aboard a narrow longboat yell at each other in

their native tongue to coordinate their efforts in removing and stowing the main mast in the bottom of the hull. With that task completed they eventually ready the oars. The dock hands let slip the mooring ropes and the people with the dark pink complexion begin their long journey home. Liveries painted on the keel reveal that these goblins live in a small community to the south, in a loose collection of settlements known as Four Villages. The rowers are held in perfect timing by the stern drummer whose methodical thumping tells them when to dip their oars and when to pull.

One of the officers leaves the docks and approaches the Bravins; it's an elderly male who seems a little unsteady on his feet. 'Greetings. My name is Culein and I'm under the authority of the Collection, may I see what you've brought to the market?'

The request confuses Yelqen as the officers would normally ask for clan name and reason of visit, but he complies. 'Certainly.'

Flipping the tarp back, he exposes the copper ingots; each one is about three feet long, one and a half feet wide, with a thickness of three inches and has been cast in the shape of an oxhide that has been stretched over a drying frame; the chosen form makes the castings easier to carry.

The officer nods. 'Very good. Uhm, what oil have you covered them in, to stop them turning green?'

'We use camelina seed,' Yelqen truthfully replies. He finds the inquiry very peculiar.

'Very good. We no longer allow ingots covered in linseed oil to enter Keties,' Culein replies and smiles. 'And may I ask the worth of your load?'

The question about the value of the cargo is the thing that sets Yelqen on edge, so he decides to lie. 'Oh, we've only one cart worth of copper this time. The others are empty because we need to take food back up to Bravin. It's been a poor harvest season for us this year.'

Culein nods profusely and pulls a scroll out of his shoulder bag which he unrolls, apparently to make sure that it is in good order, but he appears dull in the head like someone who spent all of the previous day drinking. Eventually he hands the document over. 'Good... good. Here is your trade licence. Enjoy your stay in Keties.'

Yelqen takes the scroll with both hands and bows slightly. 'Thank you, Officer.'

Suddenly Culein's warm smile vanishes, and his eyes grow cold and hard. The look on his face appears more painful than polite. 'Good...' He turns around and walks away, apparently in a hurry.

Ghun joins the younger male. 'That was peculiar.' He watches the officer disappear into the crowd that is trying to cross the bridge. 'Is that scroll worthwhile?'

Yelqen glances at the writing on the document before rolling it up again. 'It seems legal. The officer's mannerism, however, leaves a lot to ponder.'

Ghun takes the scroll and slips it into his shoulder bag. 'I'll keep hold of this.' He gives their caravan master a sidelong glance; the old male is still sitting on the mile marker talking to himself. 'I do think that this will be his last trip.'

The sun is already close to the horizon when the way ahead is cleared and the Bravin column is allowed to cross. Ghun is walking next to the Caravan Master, holding the licence at the ready for those who wish to scrutinise it. They pass the last guard tower and trundle onto the eyot where Keties is located when an officer of the Trader Collection orders them to pull to the side of the road, much to the caravan master's dislike. The wagons following the Bravin clan are also pulled over and ordered to produce the relevant documents.

Klouven squares up to the young female and demands: 'What do you want? You want to tax us more?'

Ghun pulls his fellow to one side. 'Go check the horses. Let me deal with this, please.'

'This is robbery, robbery made legal by law makers,' Klouven hisses as he storms off.

The female officer ignores the ranting male and holds out her hand. 'Trade licence, please.'

Ghun hands it over. 'Here you go.'

She unrolls the document and frowns. 'Where did you get this?'

'One of your members gave it to us.'

'This document is a forgery.'

Ghun takes a moment to let the revelation sink in. 'Apologies, but we were unaware of that, to us it seemed legitimate.'

'Who took possession of this?' The female officer asks as she gestures for a nearby militant to come closer.

Yelqen steps forward. 'I did.'

'And the person who gave you this – did you not question him?'

Yelqen shakes his head. 'I saw no reason too. His attire was clean, fitted him well, and he had a bag full of scrolls.'

'Did he ask you anything?' she presses.

'Yes, he asked after the oil we use to guard our ingots against the onset of the bright green mould. And he enquired about how much we are carrying in terms of value.'

'What did you tell him?'

Yelqen lets out a little huff of irritability. 'Told him we used camelina oil and that we only had one cart of copper to trade.' He folds his arms. 'Don't you want to know more about the person himself?'

The officer's face betrays the frustration she feels at dealing with this issue, but she remains civil. 'I was just getting to that, but go on then.'

'He identified himself as Culein. He seemed agitated, nervous and very uneasy in his own skin, skin that appeared much older than it should be. He seemed to have had a much harder life than most of us.'

'I see,' the officer replies as she hands the forgery over to the militia member next to her. 'Burn it, we've got enough of these false scrolls to fill two wytch's huts.' She pulls a document out of her shoulder bag and unrolls it. 'This is our new licensing parchment that will get you into the market quarter.' Her eyes scan the group in front of her. 'Which one of you can write?'

All except Klouven raise a hand.

She gestures for Yelqen to follow her to a nearby table. 'You'll have to fill this in.'

He takes the quill off her, dips it in the ink pot and begins to scribble the relevant information.

'Would you recognise the individual who gave you that fake scroll?' The officer prompts. She is watching him closely

Yelqen spares her a glance. 'I would, yes. Mind telling me what this is all about?'

'Yes, I do mind. It's not your concern, you just need to fill that in and then move along.'

MOUNTAIN VILLAGE

L imma falls in beside her friend. 'Come now, dry your eyes. You'll see him soon enough.'

Isfael smiles at the comment, knowing it to be good-natured. 'True, but I still hate saying goodbye.' She pulls her tunic tighter around her shoulders. 'You should find a lover, get married. Spend your days with someone who adores you.'

'I'll do just that. When I know I can't have offspring anymore.'

Isfael's heart breaks when she hears Limma's response. 'You're serious about not passing the curse onto a child, aren't you?'

'I am.' Limma's expression turns sorrowful. 'I'd love to be a mother, but I can't be that selfish. What good would I do if I birthed a little one with such a weak heart? My aunt died in childbirth because her heart could not take it, and the child followed her a year later. The second loss made uncle Klouven really bitter... He lost his soul that day.'

'Maybe this is not the right time to talk about this.'

'You're right, we should not speak about such sorrowful things now.' Limma turns her eyes up to the peak which is shrouded in clouds. 'I'm not looking forward to that.'

Isfael is slightly confused. 'Not looking forward to what?'

'The climb ahead. I'm not interested in passing the snow line. It is always winter up there.' Limma turns her eyes back to the ground to make sure she isn't about to trip over something.

'You sound unhappy and I don't think your family history is the only reason.'

Limma slows her pace and looks around to see if anyone is within hearing distance. 'I'm thinking of leaving the village. Walk the land, see different things.'

Isfael smiles at her friend. 'You want to go and explore the world?'

'I do. Go and live in the lands to the south for a bit, among the desert tribes of the Seahal.' Her face lights up with excitement. 'Yelqen's brother told me things on his last visit, things that started me thinking.'

'Such as what?'

Limma's eyes glaze over as she disappears into her own world. 'Darffin spoke of a sea, one that consists of a fine sand. He said it was like an ocean that was brought to silence in the middle of a fierce storm. Imagine, walking on a stormy sea and not having to fear drowning, and might I add, under a blue sky that is cloudless all year.'

'Sound wonderful.' Isfael has a broad smile on her face.

'It does,' Limma replies before she notices the wytch's expression. 'What?'

'Nothing, I just find it interesting that my husband's brother would share such things with someone he doesn't really know all that well.'

Limma sounds perplexed. 'What are you getting at?'

'Nothing. Perhaps you should join Darffin on his ship, sail the rivers and coasts with him.'

'Would he allow that? I mean, I'm not a sailor. What use will I be, if not a burden?' Limma's dream seems to be dying before it even catches its first breath.

'I'm sure you'll be fine. We'll invite him over for the end-of-year festival next winter. You can feel the waters... so to speak.' Isfael puts emphasis on the last part of her response.

'Won't you miss me?'

'Of course I will, but what good is it holding you here if you're miserable. Besides, Darffin isn't tied to anyone through marriage.'

Finally the coin drops. 'I understand you now – you're trying to set me up with Yelqen's brother.'

'He likes you very much, and I think you should take the opportunity. Go, see the world, have many an adventure. Come back and share the tales of your exploits.'

One of the wagons slips off the narrow track as it tries to navigate the first tight bend, the wheel getting trapped in a cracked rock. Cathe has to work very hard to keep control of the horse as it begins to buck.

Limma lets out an exasperated sigh. 'And so it begins... at the first bend. This is the first, and there are another six-and-a-half miles of this shit to go. And at least another two dozen tight bends to navigate.'

Everyone rushes ahead to help get the cart moving again, everyone except Inus who has decided to walk up the bumpy track. He watches the others struggle with the cart while poking at his chest, wondering how the young wytch could have brought him back from the dead.

It takes a monumental effort to unstick the wheel because the cart is loaded up with large wicker baskets full to the brim with sand that has been dampened with bog-water to keep the root vegetables fresh.

They finally get the cart moving again, but none are celebrating the achievement. Instead they just slow their pace because they know what lies ahead. Halfway up the mountain another cart gets into trouble, this time it is because the load has shifted, almost toppling the vehicle over. Isfael is quick to jump up and use her body weight as a counterbalance to prevent the cart from falling over; slowly, maybe even reluctantly, the others join in to secure the cart. The young wytch takes it upon herself to clamber up so that she can rearrange the cargo and replace the old, frayed rope with a new one.

Satisfied that everything is once again secure, Isfael jumps off and hits the ground with both feet, slipping on the loose gravel. She lands awkwardly, taking the brunt of the fall on her left elbow. All of the other villagers avert their gaze and stagger away up the path, apparently not noticing that one of their own has had a mishap.

Limma is the only one who goes to aid the wytch. 'Yes, don't lend her a hand, you ungrateful buggers!'

Cathe just shakes her head as she leads her cart past; the conflict over caring for her child is clear in her eyes, but so is loyalty to the clan.

Limma snarls at the elderly female. 'Unbelievable.'

'Leave it. Don't make life unpleasant for yourself on my behalf.'

'They can suffer for all I care. Let them struggle with their ailments. Ungrateful sods.'

Isfael flexes her elbow. 'Leave it, Limma, just leave it.'

The huntress checks her friend over, brushing off the wet grit that clings to her tunic and skirt. 'You in working order? Didn't break anything?'

Isfael hisses through her teeth. 'Elbow is a bit sore, but otherwise I'm still whole,' she replies as she moves aside to allow the carts to get past, her eyes drawn to the view. 'Life is hard atop the Grand Peak, but you have to admit that views like these almost make up for it.'

Limma takes her canteen off her belt and offers it to the young wytch. 'Almost, but not quite. Not for me.'

Below them they can see the thick forest canopy stretching off into the distance, its lush green foliage having been replaced by the warm autumn colours that make it look as if the mountain was rising up out of the setting sun. Only a few green firs break up the reds, oranges and yellows that spreads across the land.

Guards posted by the tall narrow gate of the village can see something approaching, but it is hard to make out any details because of the snow being whipped around by the prevailing winds rushing over the mountain. The four archers on the palisade remove the waxed cloth wrappings that keep their bows dry and get ready to shoot. Much to the dismay of the others, one of the males orders the youngster in training to go and summon the leader of the guards.

Xes steps out of his hut and pulls the thick sheepskin cloak tight around his shoulders before ascending the ladder that goes up to the palisade walkway. 'What is it?'

'Something, or someone, coming this way,' Tyrion the Daft answers.

Xes grunts. 'You interrupted my cloak-weaving for this? What is the matter with you? Just blow the flippin horn to challenge them.'

Tyrion goes pale with worry. 'Well, I uhm.'

Xes flips the horn box open, takes the trumpet out and hands it to the youngster who has delivered the summons. 'Go on, give this a poot and see what they reply.'

The young male obliges and sends a warbling toot rolling across the mountain. Almost immediately a similar tone to that of the guard horn comes back in response.

Xes smiles. 'It's the harvesting party! Let them in.' He pats the youngster on the shoulder. 'Go tell the village that the supply carts have returned.'

The young male puts the horn back in its box and descends the nearest ladder so that he may carry out his task.

Tyrion stops the guard leader from leaving. 'I'm sorry I got you out here. Please don't be mad at me.'

Xes presses his forehead against that of his companion; he knows that the male before him is a simpleton who does not deserve to be scorned. 'I'm not mad. Just cranky. You did good in spotting them. Well done.'

The complement brings a smile to Tyrion's face. 'I have good eyes.'

'Indeed you do. Come down, get some warm mead and say hello to everyone.'

Female servants exit the long-hut, each one carrying a milkmaid's yoke with large clay pots suspended from the ends. They set the vessels down under the excessive overhang of the hut's roof to protect the warm drinks against the snowstorm. Trays stacked with wooden tankards are placed beside the pots so that the villagers can help themselves to the warm mead and keep the worst of the weather at bay. Both the chief and his wife exit their domicile to personally welcome the gathering party back; they even hand out a few tankards themselves.

Once the last of the carts has rolled in the gates are secured against any possible intruders that might try their luck.

Xes does his rounds to make sure the village is safe before heading over to the column to extend his warmest welcome. The very first person he seeks out is his sister. 'Come here.' They press their foreheads together. 'Missed you. How was the hunting?'

Isfael is glad to see her brother again. 'Missed you too.' She takes a step back. 'The forest is teeming with life. I see that winter on top of the peak is worse this year.'

He gestures at the sky. 'It is. We've already begun the clearing parties, but the snowfall is much more persistent than in the past. We're struggling to stay ahead of it.'

Cathe, who has quietly approached her children, seems uneasy in the presence of her daughter. She addresses her son: 'Hello, my Child. Come and greet your mother.'

Isfael can sense the discomfort in her mother and excuses herself. 'I'll go and see to the provisions in the medicine hut. Talk with you later.'

Xes picks up on the friction, too. 'What's that all about?'

'Worry not about that.' Cathe waves the concern off.

He eventually returns his mother's greeting but remains reserved. 'Love you, Mother, but I don't want to let it go. What is the grief between you and Isfael?'

'She... did a thing at the harvest camp.' Cathe struggles to comprehend what she is about to say, because she can't believe it herself. 'Isfael... she reached into the afterlife and drew Inus back when he had already been taken by Cariion's wolf pack.'

'That is good, is it not?' Xes's face is alive with excitement. 'That means she is a true healer!'

'Stop being stupid, Child. Your sister has shown a third

46

magical talent. She is walking on the edge of a cliff and if she falls off it, she can take half the village with her. You'd also be less enthusiastic when you see Inus' demeanour. He has become uneasy on the eyes, his face is distorted and his back is hunched. We suspect that something came back with him, something otherworldly.'

'Horse apple.'

Cathe punches her son in the chest. 'Don't use that language with me.'

Having barely felt the strike, Xes frowns and says: 'I don't believe the old tales of Doumu. I mean, how can one wytch destroy half his village just by controlling more than three magic talents all at once?'

'He became greedy and destroyed those around him by stealing their lives away.'

Once again Xes has to disagree with his mother. 'Well, I think he died because he was overburdened by his training, and most of the villagers died because there was no healer to look after their needs.'

'No matter how you interpret the past, you'd better be cautious around your sister.'

Xes shakes his head. 'Where was Doumu's village located? I'm asking because there aren't many elven settlements in these parts of the world.'

'I'm not sure. Go and look it up in the records. They're still stored in the wytch's hut in Keties.'

'Perhaps I shall. Perhaps I shall go all the way down the mountain just to see these tall tales for myself.'

'Good, just keep away from your sister until we can be sure she won't pull our souls out of our bodies by accident.'

'I'll believe that when it happens.' Xes shrugs before heading back to the gate.

With the greetings done and all of the warm mead consumed, the carts are drawn to their desired locations where the provisions are unloaded. Stewards in charge of keeping stock are hard at work, counting and checking the food as it is moved into the storerooms. Servants, under the direction of the chieftess, carry the older stock to the long-hut so that they can prepare for the coming feast by using up any provisions from the previous season.

The long-hut's off-white walls appear dirty compared to the fresh snow that has been blown in under the thatched roof. Young male servants sort through the wood stacks that are nestled under the roof's overhang. After having made notes of how much moisture they believe is left in the combustible materials they rearrange the stacks so that everything has a chance to dry out more evenly. They are very careful not to block off the narrow windows set in the walls and prevent the ingress of fresh air, for none of them want to get flogged by the chieftess.

Inside the hut, the metal worker's apprentice moves along the rafters. Her job is to take stock of the weapons that have been stowed up there and to check if any of the shields, spears or clubs have succumbed to dry rot; joining her is the carpenter's apprentice who has to inspect the thatching and beams.

Next door to the ruling hut, the stable mates clean out the building where the horses are kept; most of the muck will be dumped in the vegetable patches close to the pig pens at the north end of the village, ready for use when spring rolls around again.

The young wytch struggles to get into the medicine hut because the door has expanded just enough to bite fast in the frame. Finally it pops open and she is greeted by a waft of stale air which reminds her that the hut has been left unattended for far too long. She places the harvesting bags on the floor beside the medicine cabinet and makes her way over to the hearth; the thin layer of moisture on the cold stones glistens in the dim light coming in through the door.

'The old crone no longer comes here. She works from her home now.'

Isfael turns to face the speaker; her father is standing in the doorway, his face covered in glittering mine dust. 'She is the wytch superior, please use the correct title when talking about her.'

Beaux approaches his daughter and holds his forehead close to hers, gently laying his hand on the nape of her neck, careful not to get any of the ore dust on her. 'Love you, Child.'

She presses her head against that of her parent. 'Love you, Father. Good to see you again.'

He steps back and remarks on the dirt that has been transferred to her forehead. 'You have the stars upon you, and I think it suits you.' Then Beaux walks over to one of the bags and looks inside. 'You collected a lot.' He cracks a smile. 'I'm glad to see you back here, alive and in one piece.'

'It is good to be back.' Isfael takes a clean rag out of a side cupboard and uses it to wipe the dust off her face. 'How long since Rhonda abandoned the hut?'

'The day you left for the hunting grounds.' Beaux's tone betrays his true feelings.

Isfael can hear the disdain in his voice. 'Why the anger?'

Beaux steps closer to the medicine cabinet and runs his palm over the worktop, brushing a clump of fluff onto the floor. 'The old crone hasn't dealt with any of our ailments in weeks. There's a lot of tension in the village, folk are scared and unnerved because of it.'

'There could be other reasons for it. Perhaps it's the chieftess. I sensed her aura when we entered, and I suspect it might be a bit too far over into the purple side of the aural shine. I'll speak with her, see if there's anything I can do to recentre her spirit.' Isfael keeps her voice down, knowing full well that she is divulging some delicate information. 'Father, speak to none other of this, please.'

'My lips are sealed,' Beaux warmly replies and brushes his palms together to rid them of the cabinet dust. 'I'm pushing hard to get the old wytch removed from her post. Rhonda is no longer fit to deal with our needs.'

'Are you sure that is such a good idea?' Isfael has her reservations about forcing someone out of their position, unless that person shows utter incompetence by putting others' lives in danger. Even though she understands that her father has her best interests in mind and she loves him for his unconditional support she finds it difficult to agree with him on this point because as a wytch in training, the old healer not only instilled medical knowledge but also loyalty and respect in her. 'She's been the caring for the village's needs since before we arrived here, perhaps even since before I was born. As I understand it, she basically raised the chief.'

The expression on Beaux' face is one of disapproval. 'I know that, and that is why it's so hard to get the chief to remove the old piss pot. He obviously feels indebted to her and she knows it.' He places his hands on his hips. 'I'm sorry, my dear. You've just returned and I've already burdened you with the politics of the day. I should go back down the mine, trace that copper vein I found.'

'I understand, things are a bit rough for everyone these days.' Isfael hugs her father. 'I'll speak to the wytch superior, see how she feels about stepping down.'

'She'll just laugh you out of her hut. Rhonda has no desire to relinquish her spot next to our rulers.' Beaux breaks the hug off and walks to the door. As he reaches it he stops to have one last moment with his child. 'See you at evening meal.'

'See you at evening meal.'

Sitting in the rafters of the hut is a lone black rat, its eyes glowing with a dull, sickly green light. Its head is tilted to one side, following the young wytch with its gaze as she moves around the building. The rat watches her light a fire in the hearth before she begins to unpack the harvesting bags.

The glow fades, returning the rat's eyes to their usual glossy black sheen. The creature looks around frantically as if trying to figure out where it is before dashing off towards the nearest dark corner to get out of sight.

Isfael can hear the animal dart across the wooden beam overhead, which makes her stop what she is doing and stare at the rafters. 'I wish there were more cats up here to rid the hut of these pests.'

KETIES

After their documentation has been rectified and charges have been levied against them for accepting a falsified licence, the Bravins are finally allowed to take their goods to the market. Compacted gravel crunches under the solid wooden wheels of the heavy carts, evidence of a flourishing economy that imports chalk from the west so that they can forego the problems of having muddy tracks during the rainy season.

Almost the entire southern end of the eyot has been given over to grain, wheat, barley and spelt. The fields appear barren now that all of the harvest has been collected, but the scene of desolation belies the true value of the soil. Oxen teams are hard at work churning the rich black earth over with their simple ploughs, readying the land for the next season. Carts loaded with animal muck follow the ploughs while the youngsters standing atop the stinking mass have the unenviable task of spreading the foul-smelling crap.

The five acres of land closest to the village's first defensive ditch have been split up into six plots of an acre each, which in turn have been subdivided into six equal-sized plots, giving the herds within the enclosures enough room to graze and move. Each enclosure has been purposefully laid out to facilitate herding the animals should this be necessary. Shepherds, along with their children and hired helpers, lead their beats into temporary corrals where they comb the loose wool out while checking for ticks and fleas.

The chief of Keties himself, who had grown irate at the ever-increasing prices of the raw fleece, ordered the long-distance traders to procure the new breed of sheep, no matter the cost. The shepherds were elated and apprehensive at the same time at the prospect of having to relearn their husbandry in order to care for the new flocks; the local breed has proven to be much more robust in the colder regions. That trait, however, counts against the indigenous muttons for their coarse hair and densely packed undercoats makes them difficult to sheer and their wool a chore to process.

To the north of the centrally located village is the wild side of the eyot, where the land has been left to its own devices. The flowers and grasses, which wasted no time in reclaiming their rightful place, have created the perfect grazing habitat for the domesticated aurochs. Set amongst the scattered trees and shrubs is the large woodhenge which allows the people to track the seasons.

Yelqen falls back so that he can chat with his friend. 'How long do you think it took them to move all that ground?'

Arcim juts his chin out towards the village's defences. 'You talking about the protective earthworks that surround Keties?'

Yelqen coughs a few times. 'Dammit, I think a bug just flew into my throat.' He coughs again and then composes himself. 'Right, dammit. As I was saying. Yes, the three ditches that surround the village. Each one seems to be about a one hundred feet deep. And then they go and plant a palisade wall on there, adding another thirty feet of obstacle to an already impressive defence. And they did that three times.'

Arcim shrugs. 'I don't know. You ask me every time we come here and I still have no idea.'

'You've got to admit, it is an impressive bit of work they did. I like to ponder its construction.'

'Uh huh. Very impressive.' Arcim looks around and gestures at the distant behemoth towering over the landscape, its crown hidden in the clouds. 'What about Bravin?'

'What about it?'

Arcim huffs before he replies: 'Oh, I don't know. Our forebears went up there and dug their homes into the solid rock, inside the crater of a dead fire mountain. Perhaps their achievements are just as spectacular as the ones of the Keties folk!'

'Well, your forebears perhaps.' Yelqen smiles. 'Mine were building wattle and daub huts in the low hills of Tin while digging holes in the ground of the Dindun Forest, searching for hard silver and stumbling on its softer equivalent instead.'

'Why do you have these obscure interests?'

Yelqen shrugs. 'I don't know. I just do. My mind jumps from one interesting thing to the next... I can't help it!'

'You're a strange one, to be sure.'

'Strange means interesting,' Yelqen jabs back at his friend.

They reach the entrance to the market where another group of officers are waiting; these ones are much younger in appearance, and some of them aren't even elves.

The caravan master's demeanour betrays his annoyance when a young male spriggan approaches whose skin is a dull amber colour and his deep-set eyes appear to be blood red. His black hair hangs in long braids down to his lower back.

Once again Ghun has to step in and diffuse the situation. 'Calm yourself. He's just an attendee.'

Klouven spits on the ground. 'Don't care. Too many stops, and too many people checking if things are in order.'

The spriggan shakes the confrontation off by remaining courteous. 'May I please see your trade licence?'

Ghun hands the scroll over. 'Your Elven is exceptional.'

'Thank you.' The Spriggan's features are similar to that of a Goblin, just not as sharp and mean looking. He runs his finger over the document, stopping by each wax seal to scrutinise it. 'All in good order. My name is Emun, I'm an attendee for the Keties market. Please follow me so that we may find an empty stall for you lads.'

Ghun gives the caravan master a wide grin. 'See? Not so hard.'

When Klouven spits on the ground again, those around him turn away in disgust as spitting means cursing the land that another person treads on.

The marketplace is covered in compacted gravel, which makes it easier for the carts to roll along. Merchants from far afield are in the process of setting up their tents and stands while others are sitting around looking bored and ready to head home. The Bravins are led to an empty stall on the edge of Trader's Row.

'This is for you, lads,' Emun declares as he removes his backpack and takes out a stack of vellum sheets that are secured between to slats of hardwood; it is something the elves have never seen before.

'Interesting way of carrying your scrolls,' Arcim comments.

'Oh, this is called a ledger. The record keepers needed a new way to store their records, so they came up with this. The scrolls are protected by the hardwood covers back and front, which means there's less damage to the documents. It's a really clever invention, this.' Emun flips the ledger open. 'I'll just make a note of the date and time of your arrival… and then give you this.' He holds out his hand, presenting a copper token. 'Please return to me – or to one of my fellows – when you depart so that we may note the time you spent here and tax you appropriately.'

Klouven snaps the token up. 'We know how this works, we've been here before.'

'Oh, my apologies.' Emun is slightly taken back by the outburst.

Ghun takes the token off the old male and shoves him away while smiling at the spriggan. 'Nothing to apologise for, our friend here is tired and needs to lie down. His old bones are hurting.'

Yelqen and Arcim force the caravan master into one of the stalls by taking hold of his arms and dragging him away.

'I always thought spriggans were a nomadic people who are

now heading southwest for the winter.' Ghun tries to lighten the mood by feigning curiosity in another culture.

'Spriggans are nomadic. I just got stuck here when I fell in love with a she-goblin.'

Ghun smiles. 'I take it she lives here permanently.'

'Indeed she does.' Emun puts the ledger away and bows to show his respect. 'Distinguished elves, I bid you farewell and hope your trade endeavours bear you many fruits.'

Ghun returns the gesture, clearly impressed by the young nomad who has given up his traditional lifestyle.

'Well, that could've gone a lot smoother,' Yelqen comments as he rejoins his comrade.

'Indeed. I think this will definitely be Klouven's last trip with us. His embarrassing behaviour is getting out of hand.'

As if to prove them right, the caravan master storms past them, his coin pouch grasped in his hand. 'Out of my way! I've business to attend to.'

'Off he goes to the brothels. Dirty old bugger.' Yelqen shakes his head at the display.

'Let the prostitutes remove his bitterness! Better there than here!' Arcim states.

Faulk ads: 'Wonder how many children he has left behind in those two whore-huts.'

'None. He only carouses the human females,' Menim explains in a carefree way while unloading the tent poles.

The comment tickles Arcim's curiosity. 'Care to elaborate on that?'

Menim stares blankly at the other male. 'Elaborate what?'

'How you know his taste in females!'

'Because I asked him about it a while back. Do you not speak with your fellow villagers?'

Yelqen cracks a smile. 'Not about the people they have sex with.'

'Anyway... we must get these tents set up.' Menim, who seems embarrassed by the conversation, interjects.

Arcim winks at the other male. 'Would you like to know how

my lover and myself go about doing things?'

Menim rolls his eyes and decides to face the teasing down. 'Go on then. Tell me all the dirty little details.'

The comeback makes Arcim speechless, whilst Yelqen burst out laughing. 'By the grace of Nammu, that took the wind out of your sails.'

'Enough horsing around, all of you. Let's put these tents up now so we can all go for a beer.'

'Oh damn.' Fauk's voice makes them stop what they are doing.

'What? What's that "oh damn" all about? Klouven coming back?' Ghun starts scanning their surroundings.

'It's nothing.' Fauk gives them a wry smile and pulls a long narrow bag out of the cart. 'I thought I had loaded the beer straws on the wrong wagon.'

'That's a mean joke to play on us! Soulless even. You are cold-hearted, my friend… cold like stone in winter.' Ghun remarks.

Tired from the long day, most of the Bravins settle in for the night while keeping their goods under eye. The few younger males who are not so keen on sitting still make their way over to the public square where the drinking huts are located. Yelqen and his best friend lead the way, both of them exited to have some of the exotic beers that the foreign brewers create.

The market quarter is a bustling place where all manner of races mingle. They have come to exchange the surplus of their goods for items they can't procure in their own lands or cultures. Goblins with their array of raspberry skin tones are the most numerous amongst the gathering of foreigners; their sharp pixie features make them appear perpetually annoyed and disgusted, although their laughter speaks of pleasure and joviality.

Probably the second most numerous group are the Albei from Four Villages. Their ivory white skins seem to glisten in any light, especially the tops of their heads for they have no hair. Every movement the Albei make gives them the appearance of a magic practitioner under the influence of some very potent mushrooms.

Several spriggans are huddled around a cauldron of beer, sipping the fermented liquid through their long copper straws; they look nervous and unsure of their surroundings.

The Bravin elves continue on to their favourite drinking hut, passing the brothel they know the caravan master to be holed up in. Yelqen notices three figures in a narrow passage way, one of them is wearing a thick cloak with a large hood that conceals his face; the hooded figure appears nervous, as it wrings its hands and keeps shifting its weight from one foot to the other.

The other two are a pair of trolls. One of them sees the elf looking their way and sneers at him; with light grey skin, large facial features, black deep set eyes and rows of shark-like teeth, he has the appearance typical of his species. When Yelqen stops and returns the stare as if to challenge the troll, the creature blinks a few times and then turns his attention back to his companions, speaking with them in his native tongue.

'What's the matter?' Arcim sounds concerned.

'Nothing. Just a trollum giving me the stink eye,' Yelqen replies and begins walking again. 'Not sure what his problem is.'

'Forget him. We're here to let our hair down and get some happy juice in our bodies.' Arcim is upbeat as ever.

'Sounds good.'

'Cocky elf. Thinks himself tough.' The troll gestures at the small group of elves wandering through the market sector. 'They clearly aren't from Kutees. Look, they're dressed in ground-coloured garb. Which hole did they crawl out of?'

The cloaked figure coughs. 'Them Bruveen Clan. Them live up in...'

The troll pokes the hooded figure with his baton. 'I know where Bruveen is located. What have they brought in their carts?'

A wet cough issues forth from the cloaked figure. 'Dey has many copper skins. I think they is have large copper in mines of them. One of dey say only cart single with copper skins. I think they is lie. Many carts of them, four of six look hard for horse to draw, me think dem full by copper skins.'

'And what else?'

'Sun metal dem have many also. Year by year, Bruveen elf come, bring box for chief of Kutees. Box full with sun metal. I see box many a time in chief hut.'

A smile parts the troll's lips. 'I like the sound of that. And I'm sure the boss will also like the sound of that. What you think, Plork?'

'Why yes, I think the big boss will love that very much. The king even more so.'

Brog pokes the hooded figure again. 'What else can you tell me about those mountain dwellers and the boxes they bring your... cheef?'

'Find gems, many so. Many gems make happy chiefs and wives.' The cloaked figure croaks and holds out his shaking hands. 'Give, now please.'

'We must talk about Teen first, and what they bring to the market.' Plork taps the figure on the wrist with his baton. 'So put those shit shovels away.'

The figure coughs again. 'Teen bring many cart of soft silver. Hard silver too, such many. They have plenty riches in mines of them. Teen sell many sands to working of metal, good sand for make metal better.'

'That is good to hear,' Brog comments and nods at his companion. 'Plork, give this good fellow his lump of tar, and get him on his way. His broken Trollish is hurting my ears.'

Plork pulls a block of poppy resin from his shoulder bag and hands it over to the informant. 'Enjoy the gunk, you cretin.'

The hooded figure greedily grabs the block and scurries away, quickly swallowed up by the shadows and the crowds.

'What are we doing now?' Plork asks, and his tone suggests that he is bored with the tasks their boss has given them.

'We go back to the stall and write our reports. Come the morning, we shall send the pigeons home.'

Plork spits on the ground. 'What of that cretin who gave us the information? Shall I go and push a dagger between his ribs?'

'No need.' Brog smiles, his face lit up with malice. 'I added some aconite into the mix, you know, to liven up the taste a little. He'll be dead the moment he inhales the smoke.'

The thought of the treacherous elf meeting such a terrible demise makes Plork laugh. 'I love it. He just wants to forget his miserable life for a moment but instead, he ends up among his miserable ancestors!'

It is late at night and large braziers cast their flickering light in all directions, the flames whipped around by the wind to make the shadows dance. The drunk Bravins have decided that the time has come to head back to the south end of the market quarter for a good night's sleep, yet they find their way obstructed by a group of gamblers who have gathered around to play an impromptu game of dice. Two of the players get into a scuffle which quickly devolves into a fistfight; one of them is a human male facing off against a goblin who stands a whole head taller. Those closest to the brawlers step away to make space for them and immediately begin to post bets on a possible outcome. Yelqen, however, finds it disgusting that people would put down coin instead of preventing the onset of violence, so he goes to intervene. The flash of a blade spurs him to move quicker and break up the fight.

'Enough! It is to stop!'

The goblin shoves the young elf and asks: 'Po geweg ouj kreeb mokom?'

'You tongue me not speak. Trader Common is you to use. Dis is trade ground,' Yelqen replies. He bends down and retrieves a dagger from the mud.

The goblin squares up to the elf and looks him straight in the eye. 'Teg mer asdim.'

Then another goblin steps out of the crowd. 'Him ask why you make stop de fight? Then him say him will knock you down.'

'Him pull blade, him want make fist fight into stab fight.' Yelqen holds the dagger out for all to see, refusing to back down from the person who is trying to intimidate him.

'Nagma. Neews gidouvne po ouha. Eide sseme tui teh ym sokko lavag.' The angry goblin wipes the sweat away with his sleeve.

'Him says you stop be stupid, dagger fell out holder.' The goblin acting as translator relays the words, but he sounds dubious of the claim.

His eyes never leaving the brawler facing him, Yelqen shakes his head. 'Not make me look fool. Me have eyes. Me see truth of matter. You not honest, make for gut shot with blade.'

'Geh, ien raawe ien.'

'Him say not true what you say,' the translator explains. Everyone present can hear the doubt in his voice.

Yelqen lets out a sigh of irritability as he hands the weapon back. 'Be gone. Lie does you. Not honest when fight, not honest when trade.'

As an insult, the fighter puts an index finger next to his nose and storms off, sparing the human a hateful glare before melting away in the dispersing crowd.

Yelqen clasps his hands together and lowers his head at the other goblin. 'For you aid, you have me thanks.'

The translator smiles as he gives a slight bow, a sign of respect used by the elves. 'Tradition of goblin respect, this you know. Good it is.'

'Tradition of elf respect, this you know. Good it is.' Yelqen echoes in the strange trader's language that was born out of necessity hundreds of years ago.

'Good we learn culture of others. Go well, wonderful person.' The goblin smiles and leaves.

'Go well, good fellow!' Yelqen shouts.

Arcim looks around before he turns towards his companion and asks: 'Where did that human man go?'

'He must've done a dash when everyone else left.' Yelqen straightens his tunic. 'It's not important, just as long as he's alive. Come, I'm drunk and tired and bloated. Time for some rest.'

Arcim nods. 'Yes, rest sounds good. Perhaps I'll remember

my name in the morning.' He staggers towards their stall and mumbles: 'I miss Seif, I miss his arms around me.'

HEALER

A new day dawns and Isfael is woken up by the knocker-upper who goes from door to door, banging on each one with a heavy wooden club. The young wytch uses a smouldering hoof fungus to light the small oil lamps suspended from the rafters. Droplets of condensation glisten in the flickering light where the bare rock peeks through the gaps between the wall drapes. Downstairs she can hear her parents, yawning and groaning, sharing sweet words of love with one another.

Rubbing the sleep from her eyes she squats down over her chamber pot to empty her bowels. Then she pops the wooden lid on to contain the smell and quickly opens the vents in the ceiling; clever engineering by the village founders makes use of the long narrow cracks that permeate the crater wall, funnelling the fresh air into the huts. Shuttered vents above the windows allow for descent through draught when opened, to dry the interior and reduce the moisture created by daily living.

The young wytch heads downstairs, greeting her parents on the way past while collecting their chamber pot; only Beaux gives a joyous response. Isfael steps outside so that she can set both thunder-mugs on their pedestal, ready for collection by the piss monger, but she is forced to dig the wooden stand out first. A thick blanket of snow covers the whole village and more keeps pouring out of the heavens. Somewhere nearby the keep-clear teams are busy shovelling snow into their carts to make pathways, but their efforts are ultimately in vain. Isfael takes the sights in; she has never seen the weather so unforgiving this early in the year. The cold forces her back inside.

Beaux is glaring at his wife while waiting for his daughter to go upstairs again before he says anything. 'Why are you so cold towards your child, our child?'

'She... committed a magic that none of us has ever heard of. She raised someone from the dead.' Cathe keeps her voice low.

'And you know this how?'

Cathe locks eyes with her husband. 'Because Isfael said as much. She told her helpers that Inus' heart had failed. And then they witnessed her using some new sort of magic... wind or something to bring him back. It's her third talent... How long before she reaches for the next talent and in doing so stumbles over into the darkness, killing herself and all of us?'

Beaux scowls at his wife in disbelief. 'She raises someone from the dead and you're upset about that? I think it should be celebrated!'

'You and your son are both idiots;' Cathe hisses while tying a hair net to her head, annoyed by the fact that he fails to see the seriousness of the situation.

'He's half your son, so he's half your idiot.'

She throws her hands up and storms off towards the hearth located in the middle of the hut. 'I'm making morning meal, you helping or not?'

Beaux approaches his wife who is trying to get a fire going. He takes hold of her hand and pulls her into an embrace, despite her best efforts to break free. 'We must not fight over such things. Our children have come into their own and become influential people in the village politics – well, at least Isfael has. We should be proud of their achievements.'

Cathe is exasperated. 'I fear that Isfael might be drawing too close to the edge of no return. I don't want her to become a legend in that respect, like Doumu. Only the worst people in history are remembered with such vehement disrespect.'

'I beg to differ,' Beaux replies and lets go of his wife. 'There's Maruhn, a legendary fighter. During the eyot clashes he single-handedly killed ten goblins. If not for him and his leadership, Keties would not be an elven village.'

'Yes, but he is not regarded with the same amount of disdain as the one who destroyed half a village and its inhabitants.' Cathe lets out a sigh. 'Can we speak of something else? I don't want to dwell on this.'

'Then stop giving our daughter the cold shoulder.'

The polished teeth of the hardwood comb rustle ever so gently through Isfael's hair. She has heard everything her parents have said. It saddens her that her mother would shun her so severely because of a legend that no one knows the truth of. Her thoughts turn inwards, along with her contraction; she wonders if she should curb her hunger for new talents so that she can remain in Bravin and provide a stable environment for her daughter.

Isfael's eyes widen as she pops up to her full height, her heart racing, a whisper on her lips. 'I'm going to have a daughter?' She lays the comb down and places both hands on her lower abdomen, passing her mind's eye through her palms and into her womb. 'I'm going to have... a daughter. I can sense you, Child. I can feel your energy, your hunger... your growth. This is... amazing!'

The young wytch is elated at her new ability, but her joy dissipates as soon as she realises that the villagers could see it as a fourth talent, which may be an excuse to banish her. She sits down and picks the comb up again, determined to keep any new discoveries to herself.

Isfael makes her way across the village, dressed in a dull red skirt and double layered tunic. Draped over her shoulders is a sheepskin cloak secured by a silver brooch with the sign of a healer embossed on it, a mistletoe branch with two leaves flanking two round berries.

Only a few villagers greet her on their way past. She asks herself whether they may not have heard the tales of her deeds yet, or if they simply don't care about legends. Passing the long-hut where the ruling family resides, she can feel her mood dip very low, a clear sign that the chieftess will be calling on her aid very soon. Waiting outside the medicine hut is a female weaver named Moeky who carries a nestling on her hip.

'Morning, Moeky!' Isfael calls when she notices the child's bare feet. 'Where are his shoes?'

'He has outgrown them. Not to worry, the leather worker's apprentice is making him a new pair.' Moeky brushes the snowflakes out of her hair as she steps into the hut and makes her way over to the large table beside the hearth. She sits her child down before she explains: 'I'm here because my Touha is not well at all. His stomach has been given him much trouble.'

Isfael takes a look at the nestling. 'How old is he now?'

Moeky leaves her son in the wytch's care and makes her way over to hearth where she begins to stack dry kindling on the glowing coals so that she can get a fire going. 'Almost six years.'

Isfael can judge the child's height to be just above the knee. 'Size-wise he's right on the cusp with the other children in the village, so his growth is good.' She looks over to the mother who is frantically working to get the fire going. 'Is everything alright? You seem unusually agitated.'

'Honestly, I'm very worried.' Little flames flicker into existence, prompting Moeky to shove more kindling on. 'This thing with my son started soon after you left for the hunting grounds. For weeks the old wytch has been plying him with bitter teas and useless chants, but her efforts did nothing to heal him.' She chucks some larger pieces of wood on the fire and leans back to avoid the smoke. 'Now it's gotten so bad that he is puking up a pink froth.'

Isfael turns her attention back to the child; his gaunt expression and extremely pale skin gives him the appearance of someone who is close to death. 'Brave nestling, your mother must be so proud of you.' She praises the child and smiles at him to keep his spirits up. 'Just pull your tunic up so I can have a look at your stomach.'

Touha obeys and shows the healer his bloated little belly; it is hard to the touch and the navel is close to popping out. Moeky gets to her feet, moving closer while biting her thumb.

Isfael utters the chant that imbues her with the healer sight, giving her eyes a dull red glow. The first thing she sees causes her to speak out in surprise. 'Oh my.'

The little boy's mother immediately draws on the words, fearing the worst outcome. 'What? What is it? Will Touha make it?'

'There is a very large colony of worms in his narrow gut. Almost all of it is full.'

Moeky is on the verge of tears. Anger and frustration dwell up within her as she exclaims: 'I can't believe it! For weeks that old hag has been telling me not to worry even though I could see my child getting worse. But we must not question the knowledge of our elders, oh no! We must respect them and all that rubbish.'

Isfael picks up on the toxicity in the other female's voice. 'No need to worry. I can deal with these parasites easily enough.'

Moeky steps up to the table. 'What can I do?'

'Hand me that bowl over there, please.' Isfael uses her best bedside voice while helping the child to pull his trousers down. 'Touha, I need you to squat for me, like when you go for a poo. Can you do that?'

The nestling complies with the request.

Isfael takes the copper bowl and slides it under the child's bottom. 'Thank you, Moeky.' She presses down on the child's belly with her index finger, uttering a new chant. 'Mother Nammu, give me dominion over your children.' She presses her finger down a little harder and moves it around to see if the worms are obeying her commands. 'They listen to me. Touha, I'm going to bring the worms out, and you'll feel the need to take a poo. When that feeling comes, I want you to just go with it. Let it out.'

Touha just nods.

'Brave child.' Isfael begins to guide the worms out. 'There are a lot of them in there.' Moments later a large clump of parasites plops out into the copper bowl. 'Very good, but we're not done yet, little nestling... here comes the next bunch.' Another clump of worms lands in the copper receptacle. 'And that brave little hunter was the last of them, well done.'

Moeky is stood to the side, her eyes large with shock. 'How many of those things can there be?'

'A lot.' Isfael lays the child flat again and checks him over. 'That's it, all of them are out. No more unwanted pests for you, Touha.' She picks the bowl up and chucks it in the fire while moving over to the medicine cabinet and getting out an old rag along with a small clay pot that has a wooden stopper in the neck. 'This ointment will prevent the little forest demons from coming back when Touha is sleeping.'

Moeky is relieved. 'Thank you, so much.'

Isfael hands the clay pot over and then gets to work cleaning the child's behind. 'Here. Apply this to his bottom before bed and first thing in the morning.'

'I don't know how to express my gratitude.'

A broad smile crosses Isfael's face. 'I'm the village healer. This is what I do.' She helps the child to get dressed. 'Feed him small bites. His stomach will be tender for a few days.'

Moeky gives the wytch a hug, and a tear runs down her cheek. 'Thank you so much.'

'I'm just glad I could help.'

Isfael is in the process of wiping the table down with diluted apple cider vinegar when the next person enters the hut and locks the door behind them. 'I'll be with you in a moment.'

'Good to see you again, young wytch.' The speaker sounds dreary.

Isfael instantly recognises the voice and turns around, giving a slight bow. 'Chieftess, welcome to the hut. How may I serve you?'

Saari walks over to one of the stools and sits down by the fire; age has begun to rob her skin of its youthful lustre, turning it matte while carving deep laugh lines either side of her mouth. The outer corners of her eyes are slanted upward and the tone of her skin is slightly darker than that of the other Bravins, indicating that her lineage comes from the grasslands to the west. 'You don't have to serve me, I come like any other person to seek healing. But the aid I require is related to my soul, not my body.'

'I'll make the tea.' Isfael walks over to the medicine cabinet and gathers the ingredients she'll need. With swift motions she pours the finely chopped plant material into the hole of a milling stone and grinds it into a fine powder.

A long sorrowful sigh rolls out of Saari's mouth. 'Thank you, I've been waiting for your return with bated breath.'

'That bad, is it?' Isfael scoops the powder into a clot bag which she closes up with a piece of yarn. The bag is chucked into a silver cauldron the size of a soup bowl, to which she adds some water before placing it next to the fire. 'This will see you right.'

'Age is making it harder for me to cope with this... village.' The last word that rolls off the chieftess's tongue is filled with disgust.

'You've not spoken to your husband about it?' Isfael asks as she sits down beside her ward, keeping an eye on the cauldron to make sure it won't boil.

'No, I haven't. I do not know how to approach him. He's always finding something to keep busy with, always writing correspondence to the other fiefdoms or going down into the mine to see the lingering riches that are waiting to be extracted.'

The wytch gives a slight shrug. 'Sounds to me like he's trying to occupy himself out of boredom.' She takes the chieftess's hand. 'I'm making the brew slightly stronger; your aura is exceptionally low this season.'

'My aura has died. You'll have to work that new magic of yours to bring it back to life.' Saari smiles. 'Just being silly, trying to see the lighter side of things.'

Isfael's expression slightly darkens. 'Most of the people avoid me, they glare at me in passing. Sneer at me from their doorways. It's frustrating.'

'Let them sneer. They'll come crawling back when their bowls ache, their heads won't stop pounding and their hearts begin to fail.' The old elf lowers her gaze. 'Oh, the Bravin curse runs deep.'

'I'd rather things weren't like this.'

'Then you should've let that ungrateful little shit die.' Saari's tone is hard; she takes a moment to reflect before she continues. 'Then again, you are not the sort of soul who would just stand by and watch others perish.'

'I guess not.' Isfael checks on the tea. 'Well, reviving Inus did prove to me that I'm on the right path. I just need to keep following it until I can find the results I'm looking for.' She gives a huff of amusement. 'And until then I guess I'll just have to put up with people's superstitions.'

'And what is that result you're looking for, young wytch?'

'To solve the curse that is killing the folk of this village. I do not suffer it, neither does my husband. Nor do you.' She points at the door of the hut. 'But all those who are descendants of the original Bravins fall ill, the ones who once lived in the harvesting camp. Not a single one of them has a healthy heart.'

'How do you know?'

Isfael taps herself on the cheek, just below the left eye. 'I've the sight, I can see the weak muscles. Perhaps I can use that to find a cure.'

'I sincerely hope you do... my children are half Bravin... half...' Saari trails off.

'That is what concerns me. Every child that's born up here shows the same heart muscle problems – no matter where the parents come from.'

'That is concerning,' Saari agrees. Her eyes are locked on the fire, her thoughts in a different place. 'Do you miss it?'

'Uhm... do I miss what?'

'Selkie, the village of your childhood?'

It takes Isfael a moment to adjust to the sudden change

in topic. 'I do, sometimes. In summer, yes, because I miss swimming in the ocean. Naked like the day I was born. What about you? Do you miss the grasslands?'

'I do, I really miss them.'

Isfael smiles as she leans over and pulls the silver cauldron away from the fire. 'I can help you deal with that feeling of loss. Hold out your cup.'

Saari presents a wooden mug carved out of a single piece of hardwood. 'Oh goody. A gift of life from my saviour.'

'I won't go that far. Enjoy your special tea!'

A cat with dark grey fur and black stripes is perched on top of the apothecary cabinet licking its front paw. Suddenly it stops its grooming ritual and observes the two elves below with its dull, sickly green eyes.

OBSERVERS

On the opposite side of the village, in direct line of sight of the medicine hut, is the wytch superior's domicile. Inside, there are no flickering candles to fight against the dark, no fire that warms the hearth. Light seeping in through the gaps around the door and window shutters is the only source of illumination. The smell of moulding food rises from the dirty pots and bowls that lay scattered throughout the living space. Sat on the damp floor beside the cold hearth is the wytch superior, her legs crossed, her walking staff gripped tight in her age-worn hands.

Rhonda opens her eyes and grins to herself. The smiling lines grow deep with pleasure, and her eyes are emanating the same sickly green light as those of the feline in the medicine hut. 'Finally I got you, Isfael. Your manipulations of the ruling family won't go unpunished. I'll make sure that you're ousted for your treachery, you and that husband of yours. No more shall you beguile the chieftess, no more will you bend her ear so that she can bend her husband's. You will not steal my position from me.'

High above the village, perched on the rim of the volcanic crater, sits a lone figure wrapped in a thick woollen cloak. It is a young male troll by the name of Muctan who has been braving the winter conditions that persist almost all year round on the tallest mountain in the region. For four days, he has been moving between a number of observation points and his hideout on the leeward side of the Great Peak, but now the worsening weather is forcing him to abandon his post, and the constant snowfall is making it impossible to see anything below.

Urine-soaked trousers crackle as the scout moves along the edge of the rim before climbing down a few feet to get to the old lava outflow where he has spent the nights in relative seclusion from the elements. The small cooking fire he has lit may not give off much warmth, but it does lift his spirits. Muctan watches the flames dance around in the turbulent air while rubbing the boar tusk around his neck, remembering his companion who didn't make it.

After having eaten the last of his rations, he climbs down the side of the Grand Peak. Cold fingers protest their use but, pushed on by the desire to impress his bosses and fellow warriors, he ignores the pain. Descending beneath the snowline marks a dramatic change in the weather, and for a moment Muctan feels as if he had just stepped into a warm summer's night.

Relieved to be out of the bitter cold he finds a ledge where he can rest and remove the thick woollen cloak before it causes too much perspiration; such a dousing of sweat will only mean disaster further down the road. There is still a long way to go, so the respite is short. Night has already settled across the land when the scout reaches the top of the scree slopes; this is not the same path he took to get up, but it is the quickest way down.

Stepping onto the loose gravel, he sinks down to mid shin and little flakes of rock worm their way into his soft leather footwear. Muctan weighs up his options: He can continue on barefoot and not deal with the stones digging into his feet, or he can ride it out until he reaches the bottom and get rid of them there.

He picks up a handful of scree material and rubs it between his palms while thinking out loud: 'This stuff is too sharp to scramble through barefoot. I'll just have to grizz it and get rid of the unwanted gremlins once I hit the forest.'

Thanks to the draw of the Earth the descent is quick and in

no time Muctan finds himself among the trees of the Co'atal Forest where he knows there are predators about. A blaiff pack took his fellow scout in the middle of the night while they were preparing to ascend the peak. Once again Muctan is forced to make a decision: find a place to hunker down for the night or head back to camp. Either way he runs the risk of falling prey to the two-legged wolves who stalk these woods.

Thick clouds cover the moon and the stars, and darkness unfolds around the troll. When all pebbles have been removed, Muctan puts his shoes back on and begins fumbling around in the undergrowth; he searches for the mile marker stone he noticed a few days back. Once he finds it he'll be able to locate the old trade route that used to run west of the mountain.

Sweeping his hand through the ferns, he smacks something hard. 'Dammit. Dammit! That hurt. Oh, by Fonolite's balls, that hurt.' He cradles his hand and waits for the stinging pain to subside before he tries pulling and twisting each finger. Except for some missing skin on the knuckles, his hand seems fine. 'Right, I guess found the stone. Now I just need to find the way marker... follow that north.'

A few paces away, he notices the large wooden arrow his companion created; the use of birch was a clever turn as the light tree bark contrasts well with the dark soil. 'Thank you, Gooba! I'll remember you for the rest of my life – however long that might be.' Somewhere off in the distance he can hear a wolf howl, or perhaps it is a blaiff that has caught his scent. The sound makes the blood freeze in his veins.

'Please don't come this way, please.' Muctan utters the plea for mercy to no one in particular and sets off at a slow jog.

It is nearly dawn when a voice speaks out of the thick undergrowth. 'Step forward one and be recognised.'

The scout stops and answers quickly to avoid getting run through. 'It is me, Muctan, scout for the advance detachment of Leiteil.'

'What is your purpose?' A large male troll steps out of the

bushes, spear held at the ready.

'I serve King Teshu of Moud.'

'Where is your fellow?'

'He gave his life to complete the mission.'

The guard gives a solemn nod. 'Was it that pack of blaiffs again?'

'Yes, it was. Gooba was taken in the middle of the night. He fought them off, buying me time to escape. His bravery allowed me to accomplish my duty.'

'Well done, that lad.' The guard ushers the young troll off the road. 'Go, get back to camp. I'm sure the bosses will want to hear what you have to say.'

The scout is exhausted, but he has a job to do and he wants to do it well. He follows an overgrown deer path along a shallow ravine, holding his arms up to stop the branches poking him in the eyes. At the end of the path is the large washout where the trolls have set up their camp. A second guard stops the scout, but when the latter gets the challenge right he eventually lets him through.

One section of the sandy clearing is taken up by the brawlers; they are the biggest, most aggressive males the war council could find. All of them are wearing very little in the way of clothing as they're practising their battle tactics, a training regime they're doing in slow time to build up their muscle memory.

Those brawlers that aren't taking part are standing by the metal worker shed where they're having their equipment adjusted to their needs. Each armour set is a bronze plate that has been hammered into shape to cover most of the fighter's torso; to save on weight and to prevent overheating during combat, they have opted for thick rawhide back plates to protect against over-shield slashing attempts. A handful of metal workers are busy putting the finishing touches on the helmets by carving distorted faces into the metal so that those who see them in the heat of battle might become unnerved.

Muctan makes his way along the gentle slope towards the cluster of simple sheds nestled among the small trees and shrubs. His selected path takes him past the infiltrators; even though they'll do most of the fighting they are the ones with the least armour, relying instead on their skills with bow and short sword. Their drills consist of perfecting their strikes, to land that first crippling blow that exposes the enemy and sets them up for the kill.

When one of the infiltrators loses his grip on the blade he is wielding the wide leaf pattern sword almost impales the underboss of the group. The profuse apologies offered up by the fighter are ignored and he is dragged away to receive his punishment. Muctan knows that such a mistake will most probably result in the young male's death, yet how it comes about is anyone's guess.

The large male in charge of the brawlers sees the scout moving through the clearing and turns to his underling. 'Carry on, Joufen. I want to go and hear what the young one has to say.'

Joufen faces his superior. 'Of course, Boen.'

They give each other a salute by raising their right fists.

The scout boss stops writing his report and looks up to see Muctan standing before him. Then he notices the large figure of the senior brawler approaching behind the scout. He gets to his feet and salutes his equal. 'Boen.'

Boen returns the salute. 'Rool.' He faces the scout. 'What have you to say about that town up there?'

Rool holds his hand out. 'Before you report, where is your mate?'

'He was taken by the local pack.' Muctan's voice is heavy with emotion.

'And still you completed the given task?' Rool enquires and inclines his head. 'You're brave – bit stupid, but brave. We'll note his death as a heroic sacrifice.'

Muctan snaps up a salute to recognise his superiors. 'Bosses, apologies for not doing this earlier.'

Rool gets his quill ready. 'What was the name of your scouting mate?'

'His name was Gooba, boss.'

'Right then.' Rool unfurls the scroll that contains the names of his fighters and makes a note of the scout's death before closing the scroll up again and leaning on his table. 'Let's hear the report.'

Muctan takes a moment to gather his thoughts and pulls a piece of blank vellum closer. 'May I, boss?'

Rool hands over his ink pot and a spare quill. 'If you must.'

The scout makes a rough drawing of what he saw. The crude compass he adds in the top right corner of the document indicates that the main entrance of the village faces towards the west. He draws in a few squares and rectangles that represent the buildings of interest.

'It looks like the kidney of a pig, just turned sideways,' Boen remarks on the shape of the town.

'It does a bit,' Muctan acknowledges while continuing to fill in the details. 'I think these elves have no idea that they live in the old crater of a fire spitter.'

'They live in a dead fire mountain?' Boen unfolds his arms and leans on the table too, his sheer weight making it creak. 'How can you be sure?'

Muctan looks at the boss of the brawlers. 'I've been to the peak of Fonolite's Kingdom. I went up seeking guidance for my life. Up there I saw the same rocks as I did in the walls surrounding Bruveen.'

'Seems we truly are doing the work of our god. He has guided our king to send us here, to reclaim his lost lands,' Boen speaks as he points at the southern wall of the crater. 'So, what are those little squares?'

'Those are their houses. They've dug them into the walls of the crater. Each house has two levels.'

'How do you know?' Rool frowns at his subordinate.

'I climbed down one night, found an empty house, went inside and had a look,' Muctan explains. He pokes at one of the little squares. 'This house has a strange door. It's blocked from the outside with a large wooden beam that has been baked in tar.' The scout draws two small rectangles close to the unusual door. 'I spent a day in this building, the horse stable. The elves take very good care of their animals. And here, just next to the horse stable, is where they keep their tamed birds.'

Boen grins as he addresses Muctan: 'You climbed down into the very town we want to claim for our king and people? You've got a set of balls on you!'

The young troll smiles while continuing to add to his drawing. 'So, the entire south wall is where they have their houses. Not sure why, because the sun never reaches their front doors, but fine. This block here is about one hundred paces from the gate, its front door almost perfectly aligned with the town entrance. This is the house of their king. I think they call it a long-hut.' Muctan draws another little square, placing it at a right angle to the main building's door. 'This is the entrance to their mine. You won't believe how much they pull out of that thing every day! Saw about three hand carts full of copper rocks in the few days I was up there.'

'Three carts in four days?' Boen lets out a short whistle. 'That is impressive.'

The scout nods and draws a few more squares along the line that represents the north wall of the crater, moving in the direction indicated as east. 'Next, they have the smelting pits, then comes the charcoal stores, then the pig-pen and then some unused house. I think the town healer is supposed to live there, but I've not seen anyone go in or come out. One of them went in on the last day I was watching them, but then the snow became too thick, so I'm not sure what was going on in there.'

'Interesting.' Rool's mind churns over the information as he taps his fingers on the table, his thick, claw-like nails making crescent moon divots in the wood. 'Could it be that their healer has perished and they've not found a replacement yet?'

Boen shrugs. 'Perhaps.'

Muctan finishes the drawing. 'Here on the very east side they have their food stores. The whole pantry was carved into solid rock. Close to the stores is their water supply, a melt water pit with a small wooden roof over it.' He adds a little square in front of the food stores. 'This building – I have no idea what that is for. Was not able to get close to have a look, there was always a person in the way.'

'Can you just throw a wild guess at its purpose?' Rool pushes.

'They have horses. So they must have carts. Best I can think of is that it's used for housing the carts.' Muctan nods to himself. 'But the stables were almost empty, so a fairly large number of people is not in the town at the moment.'

'They went off to Kutees to trade.' Boen rises to his full height again. 'We'll deal with them if and when they turn up again.'

Rool pokes at the drawing where the main gate is located. 'That will be hard to overcome and, once we get through, we have to bumble down that narrow, curved passage. A simple shield wall could stop our attack dead. Then the elves just have to lob big stones on our heads or pick us off with their bows.'

'You and your infiltrators, perhaps. My fighters can withstand such an onslaught.'

Rool traces the passage with his nail. 'How long would you say this is? How tall is that gate?'

'So the gate is about forty feet high. As for the passage, I guess it's about one hundred and thirty-five feet before you come out into the town proper.'

'Damn.' Hearing the numbers makes Boen rethink his earlier claim. 'That'll make life hard, even for my fighters.'

Rool looks over to the tent beside his little shed and roars at the occupant: 'Gabba! Can you join us, please!?'

A middle-aged male steps out into the dull autumn light; his head is hairless, unlike the rest of the trolls. 'What can I do for you, Scout Boss?'

'Do you know of any magic that can destroy a solid wooden gate?'

The wizard approaches the table, his arms folded. 'What is the gate made from?'

'A hard wood that can withstand axes, mattocks and fists.'

Rool hisses, annoyed that he has to explain something so trivial to the magic wielder.

'I can concoct some magic to weaken the wood and make it easier for your warriors to break the gate down.'

Boen holds his hand up. 'Right, get the concoction ready. We'll use it as the situation dictates.'

'What are you thinking, Boen?' Rool frowns.

Boen pokes at the square that confused the scout. 'Your underling here mentioned that this entrance was blocked from the outside with a weatherproof beam. I'm thinking they might have an escape tunnel behind that door.'

'And you base your assumption on what grounds?' Gabba rolls his hand over and over as if trying to coax the information out of the other troll.

'I base it on the fact that no one would be stupid enough to live in a hole and not give themselves a second or third way out, should the worst befall them.'

Rool nods. 'You might be right.'

'I can go back up and search for a tunnel that leads to that door, boss.' Muctan is quick to volunteer.

'No, you get something to eat and then you get to work building a sand model of that village. We must share this information with the rest of the fighters,' Rool commands and dismisses his subordinate. 'Go away now, scout. You've work to do.'

Gabba snorts loudly to dislodge the dried mucus in the back of his throat and spits it out. 'I'll go concoct that magic. If anyone needs me, I'll be in my tent.'

The two bosses salute each other and go back to what they were doing earlier.

Rool studies the crude drawing while remembering what the scout said about the town being located on top of an old fire mountain. 'We are indeed doing the will of Fonolite.'

BURNING KINGDOM

I t is early morning and most of Keties' market quarter is alive with activity as the traders disassemble their stalls, getting ready to head home and spend the winter months with their loved ones. Everything is done by torchlight as the sun is still a long way from rising.

Sitting at a large table is Emun, the attendee who welcomed the Bravin clan traders to the market two weeks ago. Five militia members and two carriers are standing next to him. Armed with spear, shield and sword the militia members' only purpose is to keep the coffer safe, whilst the carriers are there to lug the heavy table and chair around.

On the table next to the ledgers lies a sky disc which is about the size of a dinner plate. Its copper base has been allowed to develop a green patina, making the bright bronze representation of the heavenly bodies stand out in the flickering light. Together with the velum charts that the Harvesting Collective supplied, Emun uses the sky disc to ensure that his day counts are accurate.

Ghun, whose father taught him how to read the disc and vellum charts, is keeping a very close eye on the tallies to avoid overpaying.

'Your stay here costs twenty-one tulous.'

Seeing no discrepancy with the counts, Ghun nods in agreement and hands the coins over; each one is stamped with the crest of their village. 'Here you go. All there.'

Emun counts the coins and pours them into the bowl of his balance scales. He places a few silver ingots into the opposing bowl to check if the coins have been clipped or altered in any way. Satisfied that the Bravins have handed over pure silver, he pours the coins into the coffer beside him. 'Twenty-one, splendid.' He holds his hand out to the elf who paid. 'Safe journey back. I hope to see you again next season.'

Ghun shakes hands with the spriggan. 'See you next season, Emun. It's been a pleasure working with you.'

The attendee gestures for the next group of traders to approach. Dark-skinned elves from the lands to the south walk up the table and produce their own vellum charts and a sky disc representing the northern skies so that they may barter over the amount they owe. Ghun can tell by their heated voices that they had a run-in with a dishonest member of the Trade Office in the past and refuse to be swindled again. He leaves the deliberations behind and heads back to his fellows.

Two elves approach the Bravin group; one of them is guiding a horse and cart loaded with exotic sands while the other just tags along, seemingly ashamed of something.

'Ah, good of you to join us, Yelqen.' Arcim gives an exaggerated bow as he welcomes his friend.

'Thank you for being so enthusiastic about my presence,' Yelqen jabs back. 'Never knew you miss me so much every time I step out of sight.'

'I don't miss you, I miss your dumb-strength. You're good for lifting heavy things, that's all.' Arcim delivers the joke with a deadpan expression, drawing a laugh from his fellows. 'Also, you have a visitor.'

'A visitor?'

Arcim gestures at the lone human waiting in the wings. 'That man you saved from getting stabbed a few days back.'

Yelqen hands over the reins of his horse. 'Here, keep hold of this. The sands in the back cost me a chief's ransom, and I think the metal workers will be very unhappy if we lose any of it.' He approaches the human and switches to Trader Common so that they can converse. 'Greeted be you.'

The man gives an awkward bow. 'Elf, save me of death by blade.'

'Remember it I do.'

The man holds out his hand. Lying in his palm is a leather pouch about the size of a duck egg. 'Thank elf me must.'

A feeling of unease spreads through Yelqen's stomach. 'Thank me is not needed. No need for giving wealth. Me help you, life be precious.'

'Tradition of me village is pay for him or her who save life of person.' With each step the man comes closer he increases the elf's discomfort.

Sweat begins to bead on Yelqen's forehead and he can feel his heart pounding in his chest. Inadvertently he steps back a few paces to get out of the area of affect. 'I press fact that you is not need pay me. Go well, be good person.'

Unaware of Yelqen's distress, the human walks right up to his saviour and presents the pouch to the elf. 'You must to take, please. Me people not speak me if, me not make good for you help.'

Yelqen looks at the figure who is a head and half shorter than him. 'Me no can take gift.'

Then the man opens the pouch to reveal a ten-side gem that appears to be flickering from within. 'Elf take. Bona go home. Bona see woman and small ones of love with woman, thank elf me must.'

'Yelqen! Can you please finish your cultural exchanges!? We must leave!' Ghun roars in Elven.

'Please, must to take. Bona must to honour traditions of him people.'

Despite the icy sting he knows this gift will cause, Yelqen grabs it and shoves it into the purse on his belt, making sure to also take the pouch. 'Pleased with offer am I. Go well, go with peace.'

The human appears to be overcome with relief. 'Elf is good

person.' Suddenly his expression goes dark and he points at his chest while muttering in his native language.

'If man desire return of gift, then give back I can.'

'Bona... sure, you to keep,' the man declares. He avoids eye contact with the elves and turns around.

Yelqen, however, stops him from leaving. 'You say name Bona. Is Bona you?'

The man pokes at his chest again and then hurries off, his mannerisms suggesting that he has done something wrong.

'Come on, chatty mouth!'

Yelqen watches the human vanish into the crowd, unsure of what he has just witnessed. 'Coming!' The feeling of unease still lingers.

Arcim waits for his friend to draw closer so that he can shove the reigns into his hand. 'Here, yours to coo over.'

'Thank you.'

Tilting his head towards the caravan master, Arcim continues: 'I saw both of you coming to the stall at the same time. Where was the old bugger?'

'Inside one of the brothels. Three women were tending to him. Seems the old goat was in there all night,' Yelqen replies. He sounds as if he was lost in a different world.

Arcim is quick to pick up on it. 'Are you feeling unwell?'

'No... I don't know.'

'What do you mean, you don't know?' Arcim frowns.

'I don't know. I feel... good... unsettled... happy... unhappy. All in the same moment. I can't explain it. Relieved, yet dreading something bad to be lying just ahead.'

Arcim pats his friend on the shoulder. 'You'll be fine once we get home. Isfael will smile at you and you'll forget all those contradicting emotions. And I'll get to see my lovely Seif. I miss him something fierce.'

When Yelqen touches his purse, a sting reaches his fingers through the layers of cloth and he flinches. 'Yes, I need to see my wife. Forget all else.'

At the border between the Co'atal Forest and the Keties lands, the Bravins halt their caravan and arm themselves with spears. Behind them the rising sun has turned the sky gold and all of them agree that the day will be a beautiful one; it might even be the last clear day before the autumn rains drench the world. Once again Klouven fails to acknowledge the eternal resting place of their ancestors, unlike the rest of the elves who yell their well wishes at the moss-covered grave markers scattered among the trees.

Another eruption sends a spray of molten rocks flying skywards before the pull of the Earth drags everything back down and turns it into a shower of fire. Towering over the mountain is the ever-present ash cloud that is continuously fed by the gases billowing out of the crater. Bolts of lightning pierce the cloud, releasing bouts of rolling thunder that add to the mountain's almost constant roar.

Watching the show of power from the window of the ruling house is Teshu, King of Moud; he is dressed in a bright blue tunic with red trousers and a thin woollen cloak secured to his shoulders by two golden broaches. 'Fonolite is angry. He rages again! Perhaps he is angry with me because I've not acted on his demands quickly enough.'

'God is not angry with you, my liege.' The high-wizard tries his best to reassure the troubled ruler. 'I've prayed to him and I don't get that sense.'

Teshu turns to face his advisor. 'Don't try to talk me down, magic wielder. I can speak with God, you cannot. You possess not the gift.'

'You are right, my King. I ask for your forgiveness.'

'I grant it.' Teshu begins pacing around the deliberations chamber, a sparsely decorated room on the east side of the ruling house. 'Four generations of prosperity. Four... and now Fonolite wishes to push us out of these lands,' he muses to himself.

A massive fireplace adorns one wall, but it has not been lit as the kingdom is struggling to procure enough firewood for every household. Long, hastily repaired cracks cover most of the walls, each one a testament to the power of their deity, the god who can move the land whenever he stirs. The king continues on his little circuit around the deliberations chamber, passing the five attendees who are tasked with keeping the records of the council gatherings.

Teshu's gaze lingers on each his advisors one by one, and all ten of them keep staring at the floor, doing their best to avoid eye contact, their thick black habits making them sweat. 'What reports have our agents delivered?'

One of the assembled wizards steps into the centre of the semi-circle and declares: 'It would appear that our inclinations were correct. The towns of Teen and Bruveen are the main sources of raw materials that flow into Kutees, and Kutees is an excellent provider of farmed foods. Bruveen is rich in copper, gold, flint and other precious stones while the sands around Teen contain both soft and hard silver. Those same sands are of great interest to our metal-working guild. Several of our agents have brought back small batches and they show to be full of the magic that makes our weapons great. Seems the elves don't realise the potential under their feet.' The wizard raises his hand slightly. 'I must also mention that Kutees is the only elf town that has a permanent fighting force.'

'Thank you, Cucoes, for that in-depth report.'

The wizard bows low before he steps back into his spot. 'All for the glory of our God and his worldly representative, my King.'

Teshu smiles at the praise his subordinate lays upon him while he ponders the information he has just received. 'If Kutees has a permanent fighting force, then that must mean they're incredibly wealthy.' He pushes the thoughts to the back of his mind and approaches the wall that serves as a map; several artists spent months depicting the lands ruled by the trolls and those to the northeast that they wish to conquer. When the king traces the crescent-moon shapes of the mountains where the elves have made their homes, a grimace of disgust pulls at his large facial features. 'We truly are doing the work of our mighty God. We must reclaim those lands in the name of Fonolite and rebuild them in our way.'

'All praise Fonolite and his representative here in our midst,' the wizards chant in unison. Thunder rolls in the background.

The king begins pacing again, following the circuit he always takes when deliberating with his school of advisors. 'Have my fighters reached their destination yet?'

'They have, my King, and they await your arrival.' The wizard hobbles into the centre while he speaks.

'Very good. I'll join them in the spring when the snows have melted away.' Teshu spins around to face the group. 'Any other reports I must be made aware of?'

'The recuperation of the northern farms is going splendidly, my King. We've managed...,' the wizard catches himself at the last second and corrects his error, '...our workers have managed to resoil most of the black earth and remove the splintering rocks. Come next planting season those lands should be ready to yield food.'

Teshu nods at the good news. 'Wonderful. What about the stores we've managed to gather up for this winter?'

Another advisor steps into the heart of the semi-circle. He seems very nervous. 'We have... just enough to see us through, should God be so graceful as to grant us an early spring.'

Teshu stops dead in his tracks and swivels round on the balls of his feet, making his woven leather slippers creak as he does so. 'What is that supposed to mean?'

The wizard who spoke can hear the irritability in the king's voice and steels his nerves before he replies: 'We can just about make it to the planting season with our current stores. But then we won't have any food to carry us through the growing season – unless we implement a very strict food control system and make sure everyone gets to eat only their share and no more.'

Instead of allowing his anger to show, the troll king remains calm. 'What of hunting and scavenging parties? Surely we can supplement our provisions with the old ways?'

'Unfortunately we can't, my King.' The wizard's voice drops a bit lower as he is about to deliver more bad news. 'The few forests that exist in our lands are dying. The rocky terrain surrounding us is dry, nothing wants to grow because the soil can't retain its moisture. Our food plants are dying off, no matter how much water the workers haul out of Scup Lake. People have quite literally been working themselves to death to build up our stores. Some have even started clearing the lake's northern shore, cutting down the sacred forest to try and free up more land, but even there the crops are failing. It's like the very water we draw is killing everything it touches.'

Teshu walks into the heart of the semi-circle and almost presses his face up against that of the speaker. 'Why do I only hear of this now? Winter will be here soon.'

The wizard fights the urge to take a step back. 'The people, they...'

Teshu pokes the wizard in the chest as a warning. 'I asked you. Do not pass the blame onto the people. You are my advisor, so you have to bring this to my attention. You. Not the people.'

The wizard lowers his head in shame. 'I... apollo...'

The king grabs him by the shoulders, his voice low and filled with suppressed rage. 'Look me in the eyes.'

Once again the wizard has to steel his nerves. 'I failed in my task.'

Teshu gives his subordinate an evil stare before he says through gritted teeth: 'I'll deal with you later.' He turns around, looking at the rest of his advisors. 'Anything else I should know? Out with it now or I'll have your heads.'

Tremendous thunder shakes the whole house, opening new and old cracks in the wall. The king screams at his advisors, screaming for them to get to safety, but they ignore his order and instead drag him outside by his magisterial garb.

Teshu tries to break free from the many hands that have him subdued. 'Release me! I must see to my wife and child!'

'That's what the chamber guards are for, my King,' one of the wizards remarks, whereupon the king punches him in the face.

'Release me! Obey your king!'

They ignore the orders and carry their leader to the open square in the heart of the town where they lie on top of him for protection. Teshu worms his way out from underneath his advisors and tries to get up, but the shaking ground makes it an impossible task. Thousands of people crowd into the open square where they seek refuge from the collapsing buildings, all of them afraid that this might be their last moments among the living.

Teshu manages to get on his knees and raises his hands towards the kingdom of their deity. 'Fonolite! God of all the world! I'm doing your will, my people are doing your will, your desires! We shall reclaim your ancient kingdom! Grant us the solidity to do so!'

Much to the people's relief, the ground under their feet stops shaking. Their eyes come to rest on the king; he truly is the voice of God on Earth.

The king is watching the mountain, admiration in his eyes. 'Thank you, God Almighty.' He has barely spoken the words when the whole north face of the mountain collapses, sending millions of cubic feet of earth, molten rock and ash crashing down onto the farms below. It is a sight that fills the king with horror as he knows that they've just lost all of the arable land they had recouped, and this time it is for good.

A wave of air, accompanied by the elevated sounds of thunder and an earthquake, smashes into Moud, destroying most of the infrastructures that survived the last tremor. The air is thick with dust and the noise of the people who scream for salvation. Cries of abandonment grow loud, cries of the end times that were foretold by the founding wizards.

'Shut up!' Teshu yells. He manages to get to his feet, storms towards a group of males who are huddled together screaming, grabs one by the hair and pulls him to his feet. 'Stop your belly aching! Grow a spine and stand up! We are trolls!' Then he points in the general direction of Fonolite's Kingdom, the mountain hidden somewhere in the cloud of dust. 'We are made of sterner stuff than this! The very power that can undo a mountain flows in our veins! Stop your pathetic mewling!' He breathes hard before he continues shouting: 'Get up, get off your hands and knees! God gave us a task, and we failed to achieve it in his time. Now he pushes us forward, he forces us to act! So act!'

One of the wizards gets to his feet. 'All praise Fonolite! All praise you, my King!'

A few of the others join in, urging those around them to chant the creed of their people.

Teshu punches the air as he shouts: 'Come on, put your hearts into it! Let God know we're worthy!'

The voices become harmonious, raising their praises up through the dust to the clearer skies above.

Teshu grins at what he has just achieved and grabs the nearest wizard; much to his disgust it is the one who delivered that terrible report earlier. 'You...' The king spits the word out. 'No, you'll do. You'll do me proud because you'll want to make amends for your last string of errors. Get your arse motivated and organise the fleet! I will sail for Keties in two days.'

The wizard bows. 'I will get it done, my King.'

'Good, now go.'

The queen approaches her husband, their young child clinging to her for dear life. 'You wish to abandon us when the world collapses?'

'I leave on a pilgrimage to reclaim the lands that God has ordained for me to reclaim.' He looks his wife in the eyes. 'I shall build a new life for us and our people.'

The queen gives a slight bow before she responds: 'I'll steer the ploughs here, keep the people motivated until our new home is ready for our arrival.'

Teshu holds his hand out, a gesture which ordains that his queen has to kneel and kiss it as a sign of respect, even the child prince has to partake in the show of respect. 'We are made of the fires that sculpted the world. We are meant to rule it all.'

COMING HOME

Vaja exits the long-hut, his arms outstretched to welcome back the last of his subjects. 'I'm glad that all of you are with us again!'

Ghun is the one who greets the chief and reports on their trading endeavours while the caravan master takes a moment to catch his breath. Most of the other villagers close in on their returning brethren, curious about the exotic goods they have brought back with them. The swarm of people makes Klouven feel trapped and desperate to escape; when he hunkers down and storms forward to get through the crowd he bumps into the young wych and almost falls over.

Isfael grabs hold of the caravan master; she can see that something isn't quite right with him. She detects a wispy pink cloud surrounding the elderly male, but most of it is missing around his chest area. 'Klouven, are you feeling unwell?'

He breaks free from the supporting hands and bats them away with meaning. 'Get your paws off me, I'm perfectly fine.'

She takes a step back and folds her arms across her chest. 'If you insist. Should you need help...'

Klouven grimaces at her. 'I won't need anything. Just leave me be.'

A few people are close enough to witness the exchange, but as they're not quite so sure what to make of it, they move away. The Caravan Master growls something under his breath and storms off, determined to get to his hut.

Isfael puts the encounter behind her and goes in search of her husband.

Vaja lets out a long loud whistle. 'People of Bravin! I invite you to my hut so that all may partake in the winter festival! Another year has come to an end and Mother Nammu will soon cover herself in a blanket of snow. We shall rejoice in her slumber, for when she wakes again and delivers us into spring, she'll bless us with new life and food aplenty!'

A cheer goes up, showing that everyone is elated at the thought of drinking mead till their heads spin and gorging themselves on the remnants of last season's harvest. Standing to one side, the wytch superior has her eyes firmly fixed on the person who is meant to replace her; she, too, saw the encounter between the young wytch and the caravan master.

Klouven passes the old wytch, barely sparing her a glance. Rhonda can see that something is not right with the old male and scurries off towards her own quarters where she closes the door and squats down in the dusk so that she can concentrate on reaching out with her magical abilities. A rat that was nibbling on a piece of soap heeds the call and abandons the cosy hiding place beneath the floorboards. It scampers through the joist notch that was cut too deep when the buildings were carved into the rock and inadvertently became a passage that joins two huts together.

Klouven secures his door and walks over to the hearth. A cold sweat is beading on his brow and an uncomfortable tingling sensation races through his limbs. 'Please, Mother Nammu, not this death. Please let me live another season to die in the forest below. Let me stumble on a hungry Co'atal-bear or a pack of blaiffs, but not like this, not by the hand of this damn curse.'

A rat scarpers down the rough wall and approaches the ailing male, its sickly green eyes watching every move as if the little pest was studying him.

'No... no, please. Not rat fodder, please Mother Nammu.' He

clutches at his chest. 'Please... please... great Mother... please.' Crippling pain wraps around his chest as the muscles of his heart contract with so much force that it causes one of the chambers to burst.

Rhonda watches the old male die through the eyes of the rat. There is no honour in his death as he exhales for the last time while defecating himself, slumped against a cold fireplace where only the echoes of his youth still linger.

It is a disheartening sight, yet the wytch superior's lips are curled over in a broad smile. 'I've got you now, little Isfael. You won't lead this village into downfall.'

Then she reaches out to a rat nesting in the house of the injured Inus and orders it to turn its eyes on the young male. 'I can see that he's not well, either. Our young wytch has a tainted hand. Very tainted. I shall expose that danger before it consumes us all.'

Yelqen follows his wife into the medicine hut and secures the door. He slowly pivots on the spot to face her, a grin on his face. 'I missed you.'

She stretches her arms out. 'Come here and love me.'

They embrace, their hands slipping under each other's clothes to explore the bodies beneath. Together they move to the back of the hut where Isfael lies down on the straw pile covered in soft animal skins, pulling her skirt up and parting her legs. Yelqen removes his trousers and lowers himself into position; both of them are grinning from ear to ear, excited at the intimacy despite having experienced it more times than they can remember.

The sex is brief, but it is exactly what they needed, a moment to affirm their love and to indulge in their lust for one another.

'We definitely need to do that again tonight.' Yelqen exhales loudly before kissing his wife and getting up so that he can make himself decent again.

'I'm holding you to that promise.' She lies there for a moment, her heart racing, her face lit up with joy. 'Can you pass me a rag, please?'

Yelqen hands her a piece of cloth before he closes his belt and adjusts his trousers. 'I have something I want to show you.'

She gets to her feet and realigns her skirt to get comfortable again, giving him a cheeky smile. 'Oh? More than you've already shown me?'

He grins at her again. 'Indeed, and it is shiny.'

'Hmm, shiny things,' she purrs and joins him by the large table. 'So, go on then, get your shiny thing out.'

Yelqen rummages through his shoulder bag and takes out a leather pouch, grimacing as he does so.

Isfael takes a step back, her face turning sour. 'What is it?'

He opens the pouch and pushes the large gem out; it lands on the table with a dull thud, laying very still. Isfael get a strong feeling that something about the gem is off, as if it existed outside of their world.

She folds her arms and shuffles from one foot to the next in discomfort. 'Where did you get that... that...disgusting thing?'

'A man by the name of Bona gave it to me, as thanks for saving his life.'

When Isfael leans in closer to get a better look at it, the gem suddenly comes to life and its innards light up with tiny lighting storms. Alarmed, the young wytch steps back and says: 'It makes me feel like vomiting. I think we should get rid of it.'

Yelqen puts the gem back in its pouch and then goes to place it in his shoulder bag.

'No... no. Put it in one of the drawers in the medicine cabinet. I don't want that thing anywhere near our hut. It's giving off an aura... a vile one at that.'

Yelqen does as asked. 'You feel it that strongly?'

'Remember the fear you felt when the boar got hold of your leg a few years back?'

'I thought I was going to die – I would have, were it not for my father who saved me and your skills as a healer.' Yelqen rubs his hands together to try and rid them of the gem's touch. 'I apologise, I should've known that you'd spur the effects of that thing much more than I.'

Isfael shudders. 'Forget about it. Just leave it in the drawer, you can take it back to Keties next season and give it to someone else. Or just throw it in the Liyko River.'

A realisation comes to Yelqen. 'The man seemed… eager to rid himself of this stone, desperate almost!'

'I can see why. You think that thing had him on edge?'

'I'm not sure. Perhaps he too was made to feel uncomfortable by it?' Yelqen gives a slight shrug.

Isfael remembers something she once read in a vellum scroll. 'Wait, humans are normally dull towards magic, are they not? This Bona man must've been very gifted.' A shudder flits down her spine, prompting her to walk over to the hearth and stir the coals with a bronze poker. 'Did he tell you where he got the gem?'

Yelqen shakes his head. 'No. He scampered off before I could ask. Everyone was keen to get home, and so was I to be honest. I felt uneasy looking at the stone, but I was looking forward to seeing you again and pushed the encounter with the human to the back of my mind. When I dragged Klouven out of that brothel he didn't look his best either, so getting back here was a matter of urgency.'

At the mention of the caravan master the young wytch's eyes glaze over and she whispers: 'I suspect that Klouven might be standing in the forest, waiting for Cariion's wolf pack. I touched him earlier just when you came back… his light was… dull… flickering.'

Yelqen walks closer to his wife. 'His light?'

She folds her arms, unsure of how much she should divulge. 'I don't really fancy talking about it.'

'You'll have to – now that you've dropped the onion.'

Isfael lets out a sigh. 'Earlier this week I began seeing a light around people, like wispy pink clouds for happy folks and darker reds for unhappy ones. At first it confused me: I thought my eyes were failing. But then I remembered that my grandmother had the same gift. She called it the life-light. Rhonda's old mentor called it an aura.' She brushes a few stray hairs out of her face.

'Took me a few hours to get to grips with controlling the new talent, nothing spectacular.'

'Right... shit.' Yelqen's voice is low and filled with concern. 'Do you think it's your fourth talent? If it is, people won't like that very much.'

'It's my fifth.'

He looks at her, his eyes large with shock. 'What?'

'I keep discerning new talents within myself. About a week and half back I was combing my hair, listening to Mother and Father arguing over my abilities. It upset me, so I turned my focus towards our child, and I felt her. I felt her force, I felt the way she is growing inside me, the way she is forming.'

Yelqen gawps at his wife. 'I'm going to have a daughter?' He smiles. 'I'm going to have a daughter.'

'And...'

The smile vanishes. 'And I can't speak of it to anyone.' He bangs his fists on the table. 'These stupid legends about magic talents. You're becoming a legend in your own time and yet you have to hide it... or risk being treated like an outcast.'

Isfael leans her head on her husband's shoulder. 'Don't get so upset.'

'Would you leave this place if it came to that?'

She shakes her head. 'I'm not sure. Rhonda is close to becoming an old wytch and once that happens, there'll be no one to care for the villagers. I can't abandon them, not now.'

'You've got a big soft heart and you are the most selfless person I've ever met.' Yelqen pulls his wife close. 'Just know that I'll become an outcast beside you should your talents be discovered.'

'Love you, my brave hunter.' Isfael kisses him.

'Love you too.'

Someone bangs on the door of the hut, startling Yelqen. 'Oh damn. 'We've been stood here kenudeling for so long we forgot about the rest of the people.'

'I'd say it was worth it, wouldn't you?' Isfael winks at him before checking herself over and heading for the door to unblock it. 'See you home once I'm done for the day.'

Yelqen picks his bags up, casting one last eye at the drawer with the gem in it. 'See you back home. I'll lend a hand with evening meal.'

A villager by the name of Vukka steps into the hut and gives a slight bow at the occupants. 'Wytch, hunter.'

'Hello there.' Yelqen pats the young male on the shoulder. 'I'll leave you to it.'

Isfael waves her husband off and then faces her ward. 'So, what can I help you with?'

Vukka points at his stomach. 'I need my chamber pot every few counts. I've not been down the mines all day because I just can't. It's been going since this morning – I was unsure if I should've come sooner.'

Isfael keeps her tone light. 'No worries, you're here now.'

Freezing wind howls across the mountain, smashing the delicate snowflakes against the unmovable rocks, piling them high against the edges of the crater and walls of the few buildings that are situated out in the open. A few souls move through the village with their large shovels and scoop the snow drifts into their wagons so that they may haul it away. The only other Bravins who are still awake are the gate guards; a few of them watch the approach while the rest take turns getting some rest or go out to check on the braziers, restocking and relighting them as necessary.

Nestled on her bed of straw and skins, Isfael is tossing and turning; her dreams have drawn her into a world of unrest and fear. She finds herself in a village that is somehow familiar, yet unfamiliar at the same time. One side is hemmed in by an impossibly tall, smooth cliff face that almost encircles the village, while other is blocked by a burning forest; huts set on stilts spew flames out of their windows and doors. Elf-like figures dance around in the flames, screaming as they crumble to ash. People clad in metal armour reminiscent of fish scales move between the buildings, their war clubs glistening with blood, blood that is drawn from the skulls of the weak and the innocent.

Isfael screams at the sight, her voice muffled like those of the people being attacked.

A group runs through the fire and engages with the murderers, their cries of loss fuelling every blow of their clubs. The counterattack is voracious, but it comes too late for the females and the children whose desiccated corpses lie scattered across the ground.

One of the elf-like males stops hitting the defeated foe and snaps his head up. He is looking right at Isfael and strides in her direction. 'Yj, si kov ed eiw.'

She can't be entirely sure, but his tone suggests that he is asking her a question. 'Stay back!' she commands, grabs a blood-soaked club out of a dead female's hand and gets ready to defend herself. 'I know how to use this! Get back!'

'Nadaan yj mok raaw.'

Isfael keeps backing away until she finds herself cornered. 'Leave me!'

'Yj si ed eiw!' He parries her strikes and grabs hold of her arm. 'Yj si ed eiw!'

She screams out in pain as the touch is blisteringly cold. 'Yelqen!'

'Yj si ed eiw! Ym droowtna!'

'Isfael.' A voice echoes down out of the burning heavens.

'Yelqen!'

'You're having a bad dream.'

She tries to break away from the hand gripping her arm. 'Let me go! You're hurting me!'

The figure looks at the spot where his hand is. 'Eihn delrew eid nav si yj. Rednaltui si n' yj. Neis ne rooh, ym yj raama. Pooja si raada.' He lets go of her and walks away, entering one of the burning huts to be consumed by the flames

'Isfael, can you hear me?'

When she opens her eyes her husband's face appears and she asks: 'What happened?'

'You've been tossing and turning all night long, even kicked and punched me on a few occasions.' Yelqen is knelt down beside their bed.

'I did?'

'Yes,' he replies as he gets up and closes his dress to keep the cold away from his skin, 'I'm worried about you.'

She sits up with a groan. 'I'll be fine.'

'Sure of that? You're covered in sweat. At one point I thought you had contracted tick fever; you were sweating that much.'

Isfael checks her sleeping garment, it is damp to the touch. 'I see.'

'Should I be concerned?' Yelqen's keeps his voice low.

'No, I'm fine. It was just a bad dream.'

He kisses her on the forehead. 'I'll go downstairs and start making morning meal. You start the day how you see fit.'

She gets out of bed; dizziness and aching muscles force her to slow her movement. 'Oof. This will take a moment.'

Yelqen kisses her on the forehead again and heads downstairs.

Isfael staggers over to a nearby stool where she sits down to avoid falling over. The world around her won't stop spinning, and she experiences a sensation of falling through the floor. Something very potent has disrupted her humours. Nausea overcomes her and she needs to put her head over the chamber pot to vomit while trying to ignore her husband's early morning bowel movement.

FESTIVITIES

The villagers are doing their best to get the day's work done before the night sets in, for once that happens they'll be free to rejoice in the festivities that come with the end-of-year celebrations. Isfael treats the ailments of those who draw near to her door, despite the emotional low the dream world had left her with. A constant feeling of fear and unease permeates the medicine hut and most of the people who enter can sense it.

They try to be polite, but from the expressions on their faces Isfael can see that they've become distrustful of her and she soon learns that the wytch superior has been spreading rumours amongst anyone who would listen.

A rat watches the interactions inside the medicine hut, its glowing eyes feeding the views back to the magic wielder controlling it. Rhonda's mouth turns into a crooked grimace, assured that she finally has her former student at her mercy.

Yelqen, who is sweating profusely from helping to clear away the snow drifts, enters the medicine hut and addresses his wife: 'I heard a few birds warbling round the village and their songs told of a wytch who doesn't seem to be herself today.'

Isfael gives a gentle shake of the head while pouring a selection of dried plant material into the milling stone's top hole; turning the handle forces the herbs between the two granite wheels where they are ground into a fine powder. 'It's just the babe taking more than her fair share of my energy. Do not worry about me.'

'No, it is not the babe. You were fine yesterday, and today you look as if the wolves of Cariion are trying to drag you into the afterlife.'

'There's nothing to be concerned about, just leave the subject,' Isfael snaps at her husband.

'Yes, certainly.'

She realises what has just happened. 'I'm sorry. I didn't mean to be rude.'

'I know you didn't – it isn't in your nature,' Yelqen says and hugs her. 'Something else has brought you down. We'll find out what it is and then we'll solve it together.'

'Thank you.' She shrugs his affections off. 'Please, just give me some distance, I feel crowded.'

Angered by the fact that he can't help his wife Yelqen steps back.

She pours a measure of the powder into a silver cauldron full of hot water and dumps the rest into a small cloth bag that she closes up with a few stitches. 'I don't know what has come over me, but I should be fine once I've drunk this concoction.'

Yelqen taps his fingers on the edge of the medicine cabinet. 'Right then. Not much I can do here I think. I'll get back to mucking out the stables.' He tries to sound upbeat. 'Love you.'

'Love you.' She gives him a smile, but it looks forced.

As he picks up on it and returns the gesture, a sense of discomfort fills the gap between them and he leaves, feeling irritated and confused about why things have turned so sour.

Isfael chucks the little bag on the table and just stands there, feeling defeated and drained. Then a voice calls out to her, a whisper coming from the air itself. It calls out in a foreign tongue, the same one that spoke to her in her dream the night before.

The wytch grabs the tankard and downs the warm liquid in one go, grimacing at its bitter taste. 'There, that'll shut you up once it's entered my blood.'

Darkness falls over the mountain and everyone except the guards make their way to the long-hut where they are greeted by the smells of warm stew and mead. Large clay pots sit on the coal beads in the hearth, all of them filled to the brim with food and drink.

Vaja and Saari stand on the dais where their thrones are located. Both of them are adorned in their finest golden silk wrappings which the Bravins admire as they believe it to be magical. The embroidered edges of the garments depict animals that the Northern Elves are unfamiliar with, alluding to distant lands where mythical beasts stalk the forests. The chief has been eagerly awaiting this evening, for he can once again wear the golden skull cap with its inlay of green garnets, a gift from an eccentric old ruler who sailed up the Liyko River many, many years ago. Saari is just as excited about showing off her finery, because earlier in the year she was given a Sedie Crown crafted out of pure silver by a master smith who lives in the goblin village of Nadali, east of the Sheal Mountains. The crown's appearance is that of a bird's nest made of bare twigs that have been knitted together tightly, and the servants have done an amazing job weaving it into their mistress's pitch-black hair.

People file past the pots full of food and drink, moving towards the back of the long-hut where the ruling family waits to accept their gifts. Only parents of babies and nestlings are allowed to sit down the moment they enter; as most of their attention is taken up by their helpless offspring they are allowed to offer up their presents a little later.

Those who have already paid their respects are free to chat with their fellows over a tankard of mead. Males are dressed in the finest linen tunics and skirts they own, and thick silver or golden torcs adorn their necks, each one stamped with the emblem of their trade. The females do not sport the heavy neck jewellery; instead they wear thick leather belts that carry bronze belly discs. Although each disc has a unique depiction hammered into the metal, all of them are representations of life, death and rebirth in the realm of Mother Nammu.

Isfael and Yelqen, who are the last villagers to enter the hut, are dressed in their best too. He is wearing a long red linen dress that has small green leaves embroidered along the edges. The thick torc around his neck is made of pure copper and each ball-cap has been embossed with a tiny spear. The young wytch has chosen a self-made, off-white garment woven from cotton sedge. The dress, which consists of one large sheet of cloth that wraps around her body, is secured at the front with small copper clasps, and slits in the cloth make it possible for her to put her arms through. The thick leather belt around her hips accentuates her figure while also keeping the belly disc aloft; the indentations in the bronze are representations of mistletoe and yarrow, plants that wytches routinely use in their trade. Isfael is the only female to wear a delicate golden torc on her left wrist, its end caps having been fashioned in the shape of prayer hands to symbolise the healer's most powerful tools.

Yelqen approaches the chief and hands over a dagger. With its silvery sheen and its thin, slightly curved blade it is unlike anything anyone in Bravin has ever seen. 'For you, Chief. Crafted by a master metalworker out of the remnants of a fallen star.'

'Oh, this is amazing!' Vaja holds the dagger up and lets the light dance across the long blade to highlight the triangular crystal structure of the metal. 'It's a fine weapon,' he remarks as he checks the cutting edge by shaving the back of his hand, 'and it's sharp. Really sharp.'

Yelqen hands the chieftess a similar weapon. 'And one for the lady of the hut.'

Saari gratefully accepts it. 'Thank you, brave hunter. I shall treasure this wonderful gift.'

Isfael waits for her husband to step aside so that she may present her offering; she opens her purse and pulls out the small wooden figure of a naked female. 'An amulet, carved by myself to represent Mother Nammu, made from the wood of the old Sedie Tree that stands on the southern tip of the Keties eyot. The dormant magic that imbues this wood will slowly seep out over time and enter anything it touches. So wearing this close to your skin will prolong your life by many, many years.'

'Oh, thank you.' Vaja's eyes are large with anticipation. 'Thank you very, very much.'

The young wytch hands a similar amulet over to the chieftess, along with a small cloth bag hidden beneath the carving. 'And for you, Milady.' She winks at the other female. 'Enjoy the evening.'

Vaja notices the sly gift but says nothing about it, instead he calls one of the servants over. 'You, get this thing on me. I want to absorb as much of its magic into my body as possible.'

A young male approaches to assist his superior while the village wytch steps down from the platform and joins her husband by one of the mead pots.

Vaja shoves the amulet under his clothes and then calls for silence; the people are quick to respond by hushing. 'Once again the year has drawn to a close!'

The villagers roar, clearly elated by all they achieved in the preceding months.

Outside the wind is howling, almost as if it was already crying over the story that is about to be told. The chief gestures for the villagers to be silent before he continues: 'And on this night we must regale ourselves with the tale of our birth. Father Welkin descended down to the forest world below, where he met up with his lover Nammu, the wood nymph. They laid in the tall green grass, enjoying the sun and each other's bodies. Their passions were such that they bent the Earth and made the mountains rise up. When Father Welkin spilled his seed on the ground, he created the oceans while Mother Nammu's sweat created the rivers. Such were their passions.' He wets his lips with a swig of mead. 'But other gods walked the forests, tricksters! Malignant buggers, like Great Antler, the mythical elk god who would always interrupt the passions of Nammu and Welkin by manipulating the weather!'

'He was just jealous that none would bugger him!' Huwen screams, drawing a giggle out of the people.

It takes Vaja a moment to recover from the interruption as he struggles to contain his laugh. 'Quite you, or I'll have you mucking the stables with your hands.' The chief composes himself. 'Then Welkin set out on a hunt. His prey was to be none other than the elk god himself, for our great father had had enough of the elk's interruptions! But the elk was sly and cunning. It used its magic to conceal itself, to make itself appear as other things! Welkin didn't know of this trickery, so when he saw the great buck standing there on the banks of the Liyko River, he let fly with his arrow!' He pauses for effect. 'The great buck vanished like mist before the sun and stood in its place was Nammu! The arrow had pierced her chest!'

Several of the people gasp, enthralled by the tale.

'Welkin realised his error and ran to his lover. He plied his magic, did all he could to save his love, but the missile had gone too deep!' Vaja takes a sip of his mead. 'With the last of her strength, Nammu gave birth to a female babe and named her Elvian. Welkin cradled the babe in his arms, wailing at the world, overcome by his loss! Hearing his sobs, a lone female blaiff came. She saw the distraught god weeping over the corpse of his lover and took pity on him! The blaiff offered to raise the child as her own for she had milk to spare. Reluctantly Father Welkin handed the newborn over to the two-legged wolf, allowing her to take the child into her care, promising to keep a close eye on the beast should she get any ideas!'

'Praise the blaiffs!' someone screams at the top of their lungs.

Vaja raises his tankard and shouts: 'Ha, yes. Praise the upright wolves!' After another pause he continues his tale. 'Father Welkin dug a deep grave so that he may lay his dead lover to rest. But before he covered her in soil he drew from her breasts the last of her milk and threw it into the heavens, creating the stars and forever reminding himself of his loss and his mistake! Then he went back to his dais in the clouds and wept, giving us rain while the lingering power of Mother Nammu has caused life to flourish all across the world! She became one with the forests, rivers and seas! But our beloved mother is not complete, so she has to wrap herself in a thick blanket of cold to rest and recover. Once she has slept, she will wake and give us spring once more!'

'Rejoice in Mother Nammu's love!' Saari passionately expresses her praise, much to the delight of the villagers who get to their feet and raise their tankards above their heads.

Vaja bellows as loud as he can: 'Now eat and be merry, you wonderful bastards!'

A loud cheer goes up.

The festivities carry on into the night as everyone celebrates life and all its gifts. Young mothers congregate in the alcoves by the long-hut's main door, breastfeeding their babies while keeping an eye on the rest of the youngsters to ensure that they don't get too drunk on their watered-down mead. The older children pretend to be taking part in the celebrations, but they eventually slip away through the tall narrow windows to go in search of a quiet corner so that they can explore their lustful feelings for the opposite sex or, in some cases, the same sex.

Saari and a few of the village's most talented musicians make their way to the base of the dais where they ready themselves and check their instruments. The two tagel-harp players caress the strings with their horsehair bows, adjusting the pitch to get it just right. The four drummers, who stand close to the edge of the hearth, hold their drums over the coals to tighten the goat skins; every now then they tap the instruments to check the reverberations. Satisfied that everything is ready they go and stand next to the harp players. Saari unwraps her bell-staff and holds it out before her, giving each little brass bells a tap. The smallest of them is the size of a thimble while the largest one is as big as a clenched fist. A pair of bone flute players joins the musicians; they seem to be a little disorganised and it takes them a moment to sort themselves out.

As the chieftess begins the song of praise by tapping on the bells a hush falls over the gathered people. One by one the other instruments join in until they fill the hut with their melodious sounds. Saari waits for her signal and begins to sing, leading the rest of the village into song as they pay homage to their deity and the gifts she has bestowed on them.

The servants take this moment to exit the long-hut through the back door. They are carrying large clay vessels filled with stew and pots of warm mead outside, all of it destined for the guards who keep the village safe.

Whist the music coming from the long-hut permeates the air, the wytch superior enters the medicine hut for the first time in months, only to be greeted by a sense of fear, fear that is so powerful it causes her heart to race and the hairs on the back of her neck to stand up. Despite the feeling of impending doom, however, Rhonda's face turns into a grimacing smile as she begins to search for the source of the foul magic. She opens the drawers of the medicine cabinet, sniffing the various plants her former student uses to treat the people.

Much to her frustration nothing stands out to Rhonda and she croaks: 'There is evil here. I can feel it. What have you brought to the village, young wytch?' When she spins around she notices the long piece of wood hanging from the opposite wall. 'What is that?' Moving closer she can sense the magic aura of the object. 'Could this be it?'

Taking the thick piece of branch off the hooks, she focuses on its aura. 'No, this is Sedie magic. They're not malicious unless threatened. This is not the source I'm looking for.' She hangs the branch back up and turns her attention to the milling stones. 'What have you been mixing, young wytch?'

Rhonda sniffs the remnants of the powder. 'Got you now,' the wytch superior hisses. 'Vaja must know of this deceit.' She spits on the floor and storms off towards her own hut, desperate to rid herself of the ill atmosphere.

The song of praise draws to a close, followed by a moment of silence.

Saari wraps a piece of cloth around the bells on her music stave to quieten them. 'Listen to the wind as it howls: It's Mother singing to us her sorrowful song of loss, sacrifice and death. Come the spring, she will use the voices of the birds to serenade us with uplifting songs of life and rebirth. Praise Mother Nammu, praise her for giving us life!'

The whole village raises their tankards to their deity. 'Praise Mother Nammu for giving us life!'

'To Fermi, god of mead!' Yelqen roars with joy, much to the surprise of everyone.

'To Fermi!' The cry that rings out is followed by ruckus songs fuelled by drunken levity.

The musicians laugh as they begin to play something more uplifting to lighten the mood.

Isfael makes her way through the crowd and hands a second small pouch to the chieftess. 'Here you go, another gift for you. Use it come the morning.'

Saari presses her forehead against that of the young wytch. 'I thank you from the bottom of my heart.'

'No need to thank me,' Isfael assures her as she takes a moment to steady herself. 'I'm just practising my art, making sure the village... the villagers are healthy.'

Saari smiles at the healer. 'I'm in your debt and I do not know how to repay you.'

'There's no need to repay me. The plants grow in the forest, I just have to grind them up and give you the powder.' Isfael pats the chieftess on the shoulder. 'You are a good person. Now, please excuses me. I must go and find my husband. He needs a hug.'

Saari shoves the wytch away. 'Yes, go find your partner, you drunkard.'

Isfael gives a slight bow of the head before she staggers off.

Thick clouds prevent the moon's silver light from touching the world, but the darkness is lightened by a thin blanket of pure white snow that covers the ground. About eighty trolls whose tunics have the same colour as the snow make their way up the lower slopes of the Grand Peak. Every member of the infiltration party has a long war-bow slung over the shoulder with a quiver suspended on either hip, which allows them to carry a staggering forty-eight arrows each into combat. Nestled in the small of their backs are their close-combat weapons, short bronze swords made in the broad-leaf pattern.

A scout holding a torch marks the spot where the lightly armoured combat unit will enter the village. One by one they step around the large boulder that hides the mouth of the escape tunnel and make their way up the long narrow passage.

High above Bravin a lone figure suspended by a single stretch of rope descends into the mouth of the crater. Muctan ignores the cold wind and snow as he is driven by a sense of duty and desperation to find a new home for his people; the reports they received from Moud have filled all of them with a sense of urgency.

He touches down behind the horse stable and immediately draws his sword which is a bit longer than the ones carried by the infiltrators. A young couple holding hands exit the hay stores on the side of the building, their features lit up by the flickering torch and the romance they have found in each other. Muctan acts fast; he ends their lives by hacking at their necks and severing their spines. Satisfied that all is clear, he hangs the sword on his belt and runs over to the braced door. As the lack of use has caused the beam to get stuck it takes considerable effort to lift it, but eventually Muctan manages to move it and open the door.

The infiltrators congregate behind the stable, ignoring the dead youngsters by their feet. They notice the sounds of celebration rolling out of the main building, which makes them confident that plenty of drunk people are all crammed together in one spot.

The infiltrators' boss explains his plan. 'We split up into two groups. Muctan, you know the layout of this village best, you take these fighters with you, hug the south wall, sweep the houses to make sure they are empty. Any stragglers you find, kill them. The rest come with me. We'll take the guards from the back, kill them and get the gate open for the brawlers. All understand?'

The infiltrators clang their swords on the ground to acknowledge their orders and set off.

Those who have been tasked with clearing the village move in silence, sticking to the shadows and dousing any braziers they come across. Only a few houses have people in them, and those are dealt with quickly. The few that manage to scream go unheard thanks to the howling winds and the ruckus that come from the long-hut.

Somewhere along the way a door is flung open and two figures step out into the snowstorm, giving the trolls cause to stop and watch. By the way the two figures are gesturing at each other it becomes apparent that they are having a heated argument. One of the infiltrators gets his bow ready and is about to send a missile at one of them, but he is too slow and the couple storm off towards the main house.

'Leave them, they've not spotted us.' Muctan gestures for those who follow him to move on. 'Let's get the rest of these houses checked.'

On the other side of the Grand Peak the assault group is nearing the last of the switchback bends before the final approach to the main gate. Even though their immense fitness has carried them this far, their boss is worried that his fighters might be too tired to be truly effective. Armour bearers following behind the assault group have the unenviable task of carrying heavy bronze plates and large square shields, so they too are now spent and won't be much use in the coming clash.

Putting the worries aside, the assault boss orders his fighters to get kitted; he forces himself to stand up straight and speak with a normal tone, despite the burning muscles and shortness of breath.

Gabba flops down on the ground, heaving. 'You are mad.'

Boen pulls the wizard to his feet. 'We are all mad. Come, the king wants us to take this town and we must obey.'

After a brief pause Gabba reaches into his pack, pulls out a small clay pot and replies: 'Let me know when you want me to throw my magic concoction at the gate and I'll be there, ready.'

'Keep it those pots close, you never know how these things will turn out.' Boen hands his sword over to his armour bearers and stretches his arms out. 'Ready me for the fight.'

The wizard coughs and spits out a large glob of phlegm. 'I'd be happy to just yoik this stuff at anyone and anything – I'm not carrying it back down this cursed mountain!' He looks at Boen who shakes his head.

Thanks to the slick drills the bearers have been practising all of the brawlers are ready and formed up in no time. Boen falls in at the head of his fighters. 'Raise your shields, my beauties. Let's go and knock on that gate.'

The bearers take their place behind the main attack group; they are to protect the flanks once the fighting begins, using nothing more than bucklers, swords and short fighting spears.

FIGHT DRUNK

Yelqen stops dancing and looks around, a feeling of unease contorting his face. 'What was that?'

'That was me.' Isfael wraps her arms around his chest. 'I just wanted to hug you, you wonderful person.'

As he embraces his wife he tries to focus on her, but the mead has dulled his senses. 'No, something's not right in the village. I sense... extreme hate... anger... and fear. A lot of fear.' He politely asks Isfael to let go of him so that he might approach the chief when the front door of the long-hut is flung open and the wytch superior storms in with Inus close behind her.

Yelqen frowns. 'That right there explains some of the anger I'm sensing.'

Isfael can't help but grin as she raises her tankard to her lips. 'Easy now. She is still the superior.'

Vaja calls an end to the music, a bemused smile on his face. 'Well, thank you for finally joining us.'

'I've come to address the evil that has wormed its way into our midst, into our lives!' Rhonda strides towards the village chief with all the confidence in the world. 'To address the evil in our midst!'

'Why are you repeating yourself!? Has age made you daft!?' Beaux, who stands nearby, has a dig at the elderly wytch. 'Can't you raise this issue tomorrow, when we're all sober, you old crone? We're having fun and you're spoiling it for us.'

Yelqen approaches with a stern expression on his face. 'Chief,

I must speak with you.'

'You shall remain silent!' Rhonda screams at the hunter, her crooked finger shoved in his face. 'You who have stood by silently as your she-wolf has brought evil into our lives!'

The accusations make Isfael spit her mead out. 'Me!? What have I done?'

'Oh do not be coy! You know full well what you have done!' Everyone can hear the venom in the old female's voice.

'No, I don't. So please enlighten me – or all of us for that matter.' Isfael's tone has gone from light-hearted to defensive.

Yelqen pushes past the wytch superior and leans in close to the chief. 'Something feels wrong in the village. I think we should raise our spears.'

'You feel so strongly?' Vaja, who knows that the hunter's senses are accurate, is concerned. 'It's not just the mead?'

'No. There is a presence that is making me feel very uncomfortable, afraid even.'

Rhonda ignores the two males chatting behind her and screams at the young wytch. 'You have beguiled the chieftess! You have dulled her mind with herbs that alter her perception of the world! You whisper to her your desires when her mind is set adrift in a sea of bliss!'

When hearing the accusation Vaja immediately turns his attention from one subject to the next. 'What are you sirening about?'

'She has brought evil into our midst!'

'You've already said that!' This time it is Huwen who barks at the old healer. 'Tell us something else or piss off so we can get back to the feast!'

'That wytch brought Inus back from the afterlife. And she dragged something evil into this world by doing so!' Rhonda points at the door where the ill-looking male is leaning up against a post, still cradling his arm. 'Go on, tell them what you told me!'

Inus' pale complexion is highlighted by the sweat beading on his brow. 'I feel... unwell. I feel not myself. My mind keeps conjuring up dark images of death and pain and suffering.'

'You had a close call with Cariion's wolf pack. Anyone would feel like trodden horseshit after something like that,' Beaux explains. 'I was almost killed by a Co'atal bear when I was your age and it left me in the lurch for a month or two.'

Rhonda points her crooked finger at the chieftess. 'What of the mind-altering herbs, Saari!? Hmmm?'

The chieftess smiles as she answers: 'You're clutching at straws, you old leather bag.'

Rhonda moves her finger over to the chief. 'You've known me since your childhood. You know the powers I wield.'

'So what of them? What does that prove?' Vaja is confused.

'Use your nose. Smell the tankard your wife has been drinking from. Know for yourself that it stinks of silosilon mushrooms, crushed papaver seeds, dried salva flowers and slithers of caapi roots. All of those things combine to alter the mind of the drinker, making it more susceptible to suggestions. Isfael has been remoulding the soul of our chieftess and extorting control over her.' Rhonda points at her former student. 'And you, you speak to others, spilling the secrets which your wards have entrusted to you.'

The colour drains from Isfael's face when she realises that the wytch superior is referring to the private conversation she had with her father a week ago. Everyone standing close by can see the change in the young wytch, causing them to raise their eyebrows.

Rhonda faces the chief again. 'Go on! Check her drink!'

Vaja obliges and takes his wife's tankard, giving it a whiff. There is no mistaking the earthy scent of the mind-altering additives, and he can see the cloth bag containing the mixture at the bottom of the drinking vessel. His eyes linger on his wife's face as he hands the tankard back. 'Smells normal to me.' He waves the old healer off. 'We'll take these matters up tomorrow, once the mead isn't so thick in our blood anymore.'

Extreme discomfort pulls at Yelqen's mind, a sensation he can no longer ignore. 'Dammit! Shields up! Something evil has entered the village!' The wytch superior tries to argue him down, but he clamps a hand over her mouth and roars at his fellow villagers. 'Shields up, dammit!'

Everyone just stares at the hunter, everyone except the chief. 'What you all gawping at!? Shields up!'

Females and youngsters are hoisted up into the rafters of the long-hut where they retrieve the weapons and throw them down so that the people of Bravin can arm themselves. All of the fighting fit males head to the main door, creating a defensive line by overlapping their shields and getting their fighting spears ready. At the heart of the formation is Ghun who dictates the pace of the advance towards danger by giving a loud bark each time his leading foot strikes the floor.

The elves shuffle towards the main door where a shower of arrows slams into their shields the moment they step beyond the threshold. Two elves go down as a few arrows slip through the gaps between the shields.

'Button it up!' Ghun roars at those around him.

Several females risk injury as they move in among the defenders and drag the injured males to safety.

Nakka the butcher drops his shield when an arrow hits him in the elbow. 'Our flanks are exposed!'

'Curve round! Pull the edges in!' Ghun yells at his fellows; because of the alcohol they've consumed they are clearly struggling to be a cohesive unit.

The elves are forced to stop and hunker down when an incredible volley slams into their shields. As Nakka is hit again and crumples to the floor his first-born daughter Murhein drags him to safety before taking up his weapons.

Yelqen manages to peek out and sees something barrelling towards them, giving him cause to break rank.

'By Nammu's tits, what are you doing!?' Arcim screams at his friend.

'Some of our folk come this way!' Yelqen shouts as two blood-soaked figures tumble through the gap.

Ghun is alarmed by a wall of large square shields moving

towards them at incredible speed. 'Make it tight! Quick!'

The elves respond to the order in good time to meet the enemy charge; it is an impressive hit that almost scatters the villagers.

'By the balls of Cariion's wolfs, who are these beasts?' Beaux can't believe how strong their opponents are. A broad-leaf sword is swung over the top of his shield, almost slicing his trapezius muscle. Beaux is so enraged by the close call that he decides to return the favour and tries to strike at the crown he can see poking out over the enemy shield before him, but the cutting edge of his fighting spear simply glances off the head without drawing any blood. 'How is that possible!?'

'Are their skulls that thick!?' Another of the males yells as he tries to stab into the brow of an enemy fighter looking at him.

'I can't cut their backs! They wear some sort of protection!' Arcim chimes in. 'We can't cut them!'

'They have bronze caps on!' Yelqen narrowly avoids the tip of a sword that finds its way through the elven shield wall.

Vaja, who is at the back trying to organise his fighters, holds a short fighting spear in his hand, ready to strike at the enemies should they break through. Tame wolves eager to fight beside their masters flank the chief. As soon as the elves have pushed deeper into the building and created gaps either side of their defence, the beasts move in to capitalise on the openings and wrap their powerful jaws around the lower legs of the enemies, causing their shield line to falter and allowing the elves to regain the ground they had lost.

The attackers take a moment to deal with the wolves by slaying them and kicking their corpses to the side before reforming their wall to press the elves again.

Seeing what the wolves did brings a realisation to Vaja. 'Their shins are not covered! Go for their shins!'

Ghun relays the order. 'Stab down! Stab down!'

'Stab down!' the elven fighters echo.

The Bravins use the reach of their fighting spears to stab under the edges of the intruders' shields, plunging the brass tips into their opponents' feet and lower legs.

Screams in a foreign tongue fill the air as the front line goes down; the collapse is so quick that they don't have the time to react and are pushed out of the long-hut. Young males and females following the shield wall make short work of the invaders by stabbing them in the neck. Vaja orders that at least one be left alive, but his wish remains unfulfilled as the injured intruders refuse to give up the fight, forcing the locals to kill them in the interest of self-preservation.

The defenders are halted in their tracks when they step beyond the threshold of the hut, once again due to the extreme volley of arrows that are loosed at them.

'Inside! Brace the door!' Vaja orders his people back. 'Hurry!'

The front of the long-hut is made secure and the enemies who were left behind are checked for signs of life, yet there is none to be found.

Vaja pulls the helmet off a dead fighter. 'Trolls. Trolls? What are they doing on our mountain?'

Ghun leans up against a post. 'Well, they clearly didn't come here for the mead and stew.'

Limma approaches the chief. 'We've made the back door safe. There's a fairly large group of these buggers out there, ready to fight.'

Vaja thanks her for the update and heads to the dais. 'How are the injured looking, wytch?'

Isfael tears another strip off her dress and uses it to plug the sword wound in the gate guard's leg before answering the chief's question with a slight shake of the head. 'Everything I need is in the medicine hut.' She gestures at the incapacitated males close by. 'I need my knives to get those arrows out and my stitching kit to stop the bleeding.'

Vaja casts his eyes over the wounded. 'Can't you just pull the arrows out?'

'No. Somehow they hold fast, as if there was magic keeping them lodged where they struck, but I can't sense any.'

He leans closer to the wytch. 'Will they survive in this state?'

Once again Isfael gives a subtle shake of the head. 'I have to get to that hut.'

'No, you stay here. I'll send someone to get what you need.'

Isfael disagrees: 'But they might bring me a lot of stuff that's not required right now! I know what I need so I'm the one who is going.'

The chief rises up to his full height when he realises that the healer is correct. 'You four come here.' He calls two pairs of young males and females over to him. 'The four of you are going to accompany the wytch to the medicine hut. You keep her safe, you keep her alive.'

Isfael arms herself with a blackthorn club which she slips into the decorative belt around her waist. 'Thank you, Chief.'

Tyrion grabs hold of the wytch's clothes to stop her; two arrows protrude out of his hip. 'I'm sorry, Isfael. Xes was the first to die. Their arrows hit him many times.'

Very gently she prizes the finger off the hem of her dress. 'Thank you for letting me know, Tyrion.' Isfael looks up at her mother who is nearby. 'We'll mourn him later.'

Cathe manages to suppress her cries of despair and quietly walks over to her husband to inform him; he too has to work hard to keep control of his emotions.

The chief leads the wytch to one of the windows in the north wall. 'Wait for us to create a distraction, that way you'll be able to move without attracting attention.'

Limma joins her friend, a short sword in one hand and buckler in the other. 'I'm going with her. I can see the enemies in the dark and the snow.'

'Very good, that settles it then.' Vaja leaves the wytch and her companions to do what they must and begins delegating jobs to the people around him. 'Bring the food and the mead to the hearth. Water the drink down so it will sustain us but not add to our drunkenness. Bar all the windows with tables, except the one where the wytch has to crawl through. All of the pregnant and breast-feeding females are to gather on the dais. They must be protected at all costs.' He moves to the main door again, giving the old wytch a poisonous stare as she hunkers down behind an overturned table. 'Shield wall, form up on me. We're going to create a diversion so that the young wytch can get to her hut and back.'

Yelqen turns to leave the line. 'I'm going with her.'

Vaja stops the hunter and shoves him back. 'You'll stay exactly where you are.'

He relents, not wanting to go against his chief. 'How are we to know when she's coming back?'

The chief shouts at the wytch. 'What signal for your return!?'

'I'll whistle!' Isfael replies. 'My group is ready now!'

Vaja nods and gestures for the males to form up. Yelqen spares his wife a last glance before he braces himself behind his shield, locking it to those on either side.

The doors are flung open and the elves shuffle out under a hail of arrows which are cut short by an enemy commander screaming an order, allowing the brawlers to move closer and engage in the fight. The villagers once again manage to hold their own by stabbing at the enemies' feet, but the trolls have learned and are more than willing to return the favour.

'Keep it tight, don't get bogged down!' Ghun pulls the male to his left back. Then he roars an order to fall back. 'We buy time! Step back in an orderly manner!'

The trolls try to push their advantage when they notice the elves relent slightly, but their eagerness causes them to overreach, losing one of their own to a perfectly timed spear thrust that catches the young brawler under the arm.

Isfael and her companions step out into the freezing cold night; powdery snow spills into their dancing shoes, making them cringe at the discomfort it brings.

Limma uses her chant to imbue herself with the huntress sight. 'Dammit, it's hard to focus with all this mead in my blood.'

'I'll go first,' says Isfael, but Limma drags her back.

'Stay behind me. We can't afford to lose you.' She utters the chant again; her eyes emitting a slight yellow glow, allowing her to pierce the darkness and the falling snow. 'I see several archers, all of them are focused on the main door. The way is clear, go.'

The whole group runs across the courtyard as one, followed by the huntress with the glowing eyes.

Isfael pulls her club out and readies it. 'The door to the hut should be closed. Clearly there's someone in there.'

The youngsters who have been told to protect the young wytch draw their weapons; all are armed with some sort of wooden club. Limma is the only one who has a sword. 'I'll take two of them with me, we go round the back and climb in through one of the windows there. You and the other two go through the front and distract them.'

Isfael points at the two males. 'You are with me.'

They seem eager to get their hands blooded and smile. Limma nods at the decision and heads off with the young females.

As soon as Isfael steps over the threshold of the medicine hut she is struck by the feeling of unease, and she has to put a lot of effort into ignoring the dark aura that permeates the air. The young males accompanying her linger by the door, their senses overwhelmed by the extreme feeling of disturbance in the hut. A large roaring fire casts its yellowish light throughout the interior, feeding on the stools and the bedwear that the looters have tossed into the fireplace.

Two trolls stop ransacking the medicine cabinet to look at the female elf who enters the building. One returns to piling everything he can into a large shoulder bag while the other one approaches the local.

An unsettling grin contorts the large features of his face. 'Rieh, sno teh tawe kuku.' The bow is unslung and placed on the table, freeing the troll up for close combat, yet he doesn't draw his sword – a sign that he is confident of his warrior skills. 'Snad sno taala, eeft. Gadan kei repe, oju.'

The other troll giggles while continuing to ransack Isfael's medical supplies. 'Kei ryk deewde repe.'

The young wytch nervously adjusts her grip on the club. 'I

don't know what you two just said, but I do not like the tone at all.' Her companions are eager to prove themselves and charge in, despite the wytch calling for them to hold back. 'No! Don't rush in!'

Their hubris is dealt with quickly as the first young male is laid out with a single punch to the face that renders him unconscious. The second male is disarmed and then kicked in the groin to add insult to injury. Isfael storms in to help, but she too is overpowered in a swift manner as the troll dodges her strike, blocks the return swing and punches her in the side of the head.

A figure lunges at the troll and strikes him in the face, but the latter is not amused and makes sure to end the young elf's life by caving his skull in with his own club. After letting out a low grunt the troll drops the club next to the young male's corpse, approaches the semi-conscious healer and begins to remove her belt.

The looter grins at the prospect of seeing a naked female elf and stands there staring when he hears something behind him. Spinning around he is greeted by the tip of sword that is shoved through his guts with so much force that it severs his spine; his death is one of indecency as he defecates himself with his final breath.

Seeing his fellow warrior go down so easily enrages the first troll. He draws his sword and goes after the female who has killed his mate. Limma defends herself by swatting at her attacker, working very hard to keep him back, but his skill allows him to counter her efforts with ease. The two younger females move to help, but they are quickly brought low; one has her arm severed just above the right elbow while the other is disarmed before her knee is broken by the troll bending it the wrong way with a powerful kick.

Limma tries to capitalise on the opening her two helpers have created at great cost, but she is unable to draw blood as the troll once again shows his proficiency by parrying her strike and backing her into a corner, and her sword is finally swatted from her grasp.

The infiltrator presses the tip of his weapon against her throat and is about to push it home when an arrow punches through the back of his head, popping his eye out of its socket. No sound leaves the troll's mouth as he collapses to the floor.

Isfael is standing by the medicine cabinet, a bow in hand. 'Come, Limma. We must see to the youngsters.'

Limma retrieves her sword and goes to check on the female whose arm was lobbed off. 'Numma is dead.' She helps the other one up. 'Can you walk, Sumi?'

'My knee! It hurts and it won't move.'

'I'll carry you.'

Isfael curses the air. 'Lifa is dead and Pouta is unconscious. I can't bear him and those bags.'

Limma thinks quickly. 'Tie Pouta to my belt. I'll drag him to the long-hut. You just worry about your medical supplies.'

The wytch retrieves a long piece of rope from the far side of the hut and uses it to tie the unconscious young male to her friend's waist. 'Go, get these children to safety, I'm right behind you.'

'We go together.'

Isfael shoves her friend towards the door before approaching the dead troll by the medicine cabinet. 'Fine, just go and get ready to move. I'll arm myself with the enemy's bow and quiver so that I can give cover should the worst happen.'

'Good thinking. I'll be a nice slow target should they spot me.'

Limma steps out of the medicine hut and begins walking towards the main building. Her advance is difficult as the weight of the young male causes her to slip in the deep snow while the young female throws her off balance with each hop. They can still hear a ruckus by the main door of the long-hut, a sign that the diversion is still ongoing.

Sumi begins to struggle against the arm holding her up. 'No, let me go. Let me go.'

After having armed herself with the weapons of her enemy

Isfael leaves the medicine hut and sees the young female flopping over in the snow. 'What is the hold up?'

'I'll just crawl back! The shaking and jolting is causing more pain to my knee.'

An infiltrator notices something in the corner of his eye and looks over to see three or perhaps four figures out in the open. He whistles to his nearby mates to draw their attention, gesturing at the targets.

Limma's vision allows her to see the troll archers line up and nock their arrows. 'Isfael, old friend.'

'I see them. Go, now.' The wytch releases her first arrow and downs one of the enemies. 'Go!'

Sumi scurries away, seemingly immune to the pain of her broken knee. Limma doesn't wait around and goes after the young female, even managing to keep pace with her, despite the deadweight of the unconscious Pouta.

The enemy archers shoot back, their missiles coming close but fail to hit true. Isfael curses the accuracy of her opponents but manages to avoid getting hit by moving around between shots, making a conscious effort to draw closer to the long-hut with each step. The trolls do as they have been trained: They stand in line and loose volley after volley at their target; the two hundred feet to their opponent makes for flat shooting, but they fail to land a debilitating hit. The elf, however, draws on eighty-one years of experience hunting in the forests and makes every shot count, aware that she might not get a second chance.

Several of the servants can see the people struggling through the snow while the village healer is exchanging missiles with the enemy; they ignore their own safety and take it upon themselves to go out and offer up some help. Isfael hands her baggage over but remains in the courtyard to keep the trolls on the back foot while her fellow villagers scarper to safety.

Another troll goes down, cursing his fate, as an arrow slams into his clavicle and pierces his lung; it has become clear to the invaders that they are facing a foe who is a superior shot, so they back away, dragging their injured with them while calling for help. More archers take up position and begin launching missiles at the lone shooter, but they too are dealt a harsh lesson in accuracy and coolness under pressure. Isfael can see that her enemies have become hesitant to take her on as they just stand there, bows held at low-ready, so she takes that as her cue to break off the fight.

Back inside the long-hut, the healer removes the procured equipment and lays it aside so that she can tend to the wounded; the rush of adrenaline is countering the effects of the mead, giving her some clarity of mind. Soon she realises that the feeling of unease from the medicine hut is still gnawing at her, extending its ugly claws out to tear at her soul.

The faces of those close by support her own discomfort: A presence they too can sense has filled the atmosphere. Isfael mutters a prayer to Mother Nammu, asking her to hide the sense of dread and to help perform her duties flawlessly. When she opens her eyes and begins rummaging through the medicine bag she notices someone glaring at her from across the hut; it is the wytch superior and there is a distorted smile on her face, an expression that makes her appear malicious.

Isfael shrugs her troubles off for now and focuses on the nearest male with two arrows in his leg. 'Lie still. I need to get these things out.'

'Please don't pull on them again.'

'I won't, but I have to stick my fingers in there to see why they won't budge.' She tries to sound reassuring, but she knows the pain that her procedure will inflict. 'Ready?'

'No, no I'm not ready.'

'It has to happen, Gesta. Take a deep breath and ride it out. This is the best I can do to save your life.'

He does as he is told and closes his eyes while the healer shoves her pinkie into the wound.

Isfael is surprised by what she feels. 'There is something sharp poking me – as if the arrowhead is facing the wrong way, but on two sides.' She stops what she is doing and pulls an arrow out of the confiscated quiver. 'That is a nasty bloody design.'

Limma squats down next to her friend. 'Anything I can do to help?'

'Yes, you can. You need to hold my wards down while I pull these dastardly things out.' She shows the other female what she has discovered.

'That is a nasty shape to put in an arrowhead.'

Isfael looks around the long-hut, then her gaze halts the decorations dangling from the rafters. 'I've got an idea. Can you grab as many of those spirit wardens as you can?'

'You want me to break the wall that keeps out the evil spirits?' Limma is shocked by the young wytch's request.

'I think we have slightly more pressing matters to deal with, other than bad dreams.'

'Fine, I'll grab them for you.' Limma gets up so that she can help do what needs to be done.

Isfael cuts away the yarn and string that holds the pendants together, discarding most of them while keeping the white goose feathers. With her skinning dagger she modifies the quills and slides them over the swept-back prongs on the arrow heads inside the wound. Holding the arrow and quills stable eventually allows her to pull the missile from her patient's flesh. 'It's working! Now to stitch that shut and stop the bleeding.'

Although Gesta grunts in pain as the wytch works on him he doesn't scream, assured that his life has been saved. Isfael repeats the procedure on the rest of the injured villagers before she gets to work stitching up the sword wounds.

The males who took part in the distraction are splayed out by the main entrance, having driven the invaders back once again and securing the doors. They are checked over for injuries by the females who ply them with drink to keep their spirits up.

Trolls burst in through two windows, much to the surprise of the elves who react instantly and manage to beat them back, thanks to the barricades. A third window is breached, but to very little fanfare as the lead troll gets stuck and prevents the rest from gaining entry. Vaja grins at the trapped fighter while raising a three-legged stool above his head with which he bludgeons the enemy fighter to death. 'See, we can get through their crown covers. Just takes a bit more effort.'

Appalled by her husband's display of violence, Saari grabs hold of his arm and whispers in his ear: 'You done? The people are looking to you for guidance, so get a hold of yourself.'

After having made sure that nobody can overhear them, he retorts: 'I do have a hold of myself, I just needed that one.'

A metalworker by the name of Vouhu pulls the armour off a dead troll and looks at it. 'How did they make this? Did they hammer it out of one piece or was it cast in this shape?'

Huwen gives the dead fighter a kick. 'I'm more interested in what brought these buggers to our village.'

Vaja approaches the pair. 'Our mine, of course. The very thing that has helped us flourish has also brought this foul scourge up here.'

'This is interesting.' Indifferent to the conversation, Vouhu tries the armour on himself. 'It is heavy when picked up, but the weight melts away once you strap it to your body.'

Ghun ducks back inside amidst a shower of arrows. 'Slithering sons of a gut parasite! That was close.'

'Ghun! What are you doing?' Vaja sounds annoyed.

'I've had a little look at their numbers,' the elf replies and shakes his head, 'and it looks not good for us.'

The chief rests the tip of his spear on the chair next to him. 'Care to explain?'

'There's a lot of them out there – nearly as many fighters as we have villagers. At least half that number are clad in bronze plates and have those big shields, while the rest are bristling with arrows. We can't hope to fight them off. They've got us surrounded in here.'

Vaja looks up at the roof. 'And all they have to do is put a flame to the thatching.' He lets out a sigh, his mind working to come up with a solution, a plan to counter the enemies who are now trespassing in his domain.

'Can king of elf speak?!' A deep rumbling voice inquires after the chief, using the language known to all as Trader Common.

Vaja approaches the small window slit beside the main door. 'What want you!?'

'Who is king of elf town!?'

'Chief of village is I! Stupid ask by you! Why has trollem come by Bravin!?' Vaja grimaces at the figure standing in the flickering light of two braziers.

'Town we want! Town got we!' The negotiator sounds very sure of himself.

'You is make good! Now you is free to be leaving! Go well!' The sarcasm is thick in Vaja's response.

'Trollem king want elf king to be friend of him! We is must all be friends, work together!'

Vaja sneers. 'He wants to be friends and yet he sends his fighters to shed the blood of my people!' The chief decides to buy them some time. 'Me desire to speak with me people! I speak with trollem again soon!' He turns around and addresses the elves: 'Did you all hear that? These streaks of stomach upset have come here to make us their friends.'

'Sounds more like they want us to be their servants,' Yelqen offers up his take on the matter.

Vaja points at the hunter. 'Precisely. Call us friends but have us work our own mines to enrich them.'

'I'd rather fall under their swords than give up my freedoms.' Yelqen says out loud what everyone in the village feels.

'Same here,' a female close by shouts.

A rumble of agreement rolls through the hut.

Vaja shoves his face up to the small window beside the main door. 'Village of Bravin not for trollem to have. All trollem free to piss off!'

The negotiator grins and then translates the words, causing most of the other trolls to laugh out loud. He lets the mockery go on for a few moments before he calls for silence. 'King of elf town not smart! Trollems light roof with flame! Flame make elf people come out! Or elf to stay put, make elf to burn dead!'

'The arrogance of these horse apples.' Vaja gestures for the males to come closer. 'I want to go out there and kill as many of those toad-stools as I can. Who is with me?'

'Not I.' Ghun places a hand on the chief's shoulder. 'I'll lead a party out. Tie them down in a brawl while you escape the mountain with the younger folk. I just ask for volunteers.'

Vaja pushes the hand away. 'I'm the chief here...'

Ghun doesn't let the leader finish 'Yes, you are, and that is why it's important that you and your family survive.'

'I can't ask any of you...'

'Why is king of elf town no more speaking!?'

'For me be speaking with my kin, you shit of frog arse!' Vaja composes himself so that he may address his people again. 'I can't ask you or anyone to make that sort of sacrifice. I just can't.'

Beaux grunts at the remark. 'You don't have to ask. We'll do it willingly. Us older folks will cover your escape.'

'But you could all die,' Cathe counters her husband. 'What then?'

'I've lived a long and fruitful life and I leave behind a wonderful legacy in my daughter. You are the best wife to ever walk this world. I can die knowing peace in my heart for loving you.'

Vaja looks at the people surrounding him. 'Do all of you feel this way?'

Ghun is the first to answer. 'We do, yes.'

'All of you?'

The older males nod. Females of their age group step closer and offer to stand shoulder to shoulder with their husbands and brothers, Cathe included.

Beaux smiles and pulls his wife closer. 'Stubborn you.'

She briefly hugs him; there is no time for snide remarks or comebacks.

Vaja is overcome by emotions when he sees that almost half of his people are willing to fall on the enemy's swords and buy the others the time they need to get away to safety. The decision to abandon the village is made even harder when he realises that they have very little time to prepare. 'Very well then. You'll have to exit through the north windows and draw the intruders away from the stables so that we can make our way through to the escape tunnel.' He points at a few young males and calls them closer; they are the stable mates who have to care for the horses, and their choosing is no coincidence. 'You six, I want you to kill the horse as we go, because we are burning it down once we are out the other side. I do not want the poor creatures to suffer death by fire.'

One of the young males shakes his head. 'Must we kill them? Can't we just ride them down to the forest?'

'Yes, we must kill them, otherwise the trolls will have something to eat. And no, you can't ride them out the gate and down the mountain. Navigating the tight turns in darkness and snow will be a disaster, that's if you can even get past the enemy.'

Yelqen agreed with his chief; his tone is matter of fact. 'You'll be doing a great service to your village.'

Next Vaja faces the people close to him. 'I need one volunteer to set fire to the food stores at the far end of the village. We must leave as little as possible for the trolls.'

Harlon coughs to draw attention to himself. 'I'll do it. I'll burn the food.'

The chief claps his hands together. 'Right. We need litters to transport the injured. Break up the tables. Get them ready to go,' he commands as he moves over to the platform. 'Wytch, how many litters do we need?'

Isfael holds her hands up; they are covered in blood up to her elbows, some of it dry, some still glistening. 'Seven, Chief.'

'You've heard her. Make seven litters, work fast!' Vaja walks over to the front of the building so that he may speak to the negotiator again. 'Hear now, trollem. Speak must we of new life under chief of you!'

'What does king of elf town want know!?'

'What would trollem chief offer to us!? What is us to get out of deal with you chief!?'

The villagers get to work while their leader stalls for time. A quick reconnaissance of their exit points tells those who offered to fight as a rear guard that there is a substantial contingent of troll archers just watching the windows, which means the elves won't be able to get their shields up in time to defend against the missiles.

Beaux is quick to come up with a new plan and orders the servants to wet the wall with mead so that they can hack it apart without filling the long-hut with plaster dust.

Isfael ties the injured to their litters while also seeing to the others who can walk by themselves. She has to keep her concentration high to block out the feeling of unease that appears to be emanating from the strange gem, but now is not the time to go searching for it. The wytch superior is just as hard at work doing what she can, but because of her age-worn fingers and stiff joints she is more of a hindrance than a help.

Vaja keeps looking back to see how the preparations are going. Eventually everyone faces him, their arms crossed above their heads to show they are ready. 'Trollem must to wait! I is to chat with my kin upon agreement we do make!'

'Why king of elf town speak with people!? King must rule with hand so strong!'

Vaja spits on the ground to show his disdain for the intruders. 'Uncouth pigs.' He approaches the rear guard. 'Mother Nammu holds all of you to her breast, all of you.'

They give a bow of respect to their chief before they turn away, ready to do their duty. Vaja takes a deep breath and orders them to move out.

FIGHT HARD

The north wall of the long-hut collapses outward as the elves kick it and break the last few rods of wattle holding it in place. They emerge from underneath the thatched roof's excessive overhang, presenting the enemy archers with a barrier of shields. The infiltrators, who are taken aback by what they see, shoot arrow after arrow at the fast-advancing locals.

Several of the elves break rank and charge into the midst of shooters, engaging with them close up and spilling their black blood on the pristine snow. The trolls who aren't cut down immediately are forced to withdraw a few paces so that they can reorganise and arm themselves with their swords. Those who have broken rank slow their pace, allowing the others to help form a new shield wall and face the enemy brawlers that are coming around from the front of the building.

Ghun is the only one who keeps exposing his head as he has the same gift as his niece and is able to pierce the darkness with his hunter's sight. 'Here come their shield bearers! Get ready for the hit!'

Beaux is looking back and sees the other group coming up from the long-hut's back door. 'To our rear! Second stampede coming in!'

The elves hunker down and await the clash when an idea comes to Huwen. 'On my mark we split! Let the buggers slam their heads together!'

The defenders laugh and get ready to break ranks again. Right on cue they split into two groups, letting the trolls run headfirst into each other at a full speed. Their grunts and curses fill the air, but the impact has done little to deter them as they reform quickly and go after the elves. The rear guard reorganises into one coherent group so that they may face the invaders and perhaps even deal them a crippling blow.

Vaja, who can see that the valiant efforts of the volunteers are paying diffidence, orders his people out through the south facing windows; only a few archers have remained there to try and secure the perimeter, but they are quickly overpowered, opening the way up to escape.

The very last person to leave the long-hut is Yelqen who makes sure they have left no living people behind. Lying on the raised platform are the dead, their eyes staring into the afterlife, their souls having departed.

Harlon grabs an unlit torch from inside the stables, hunkers down by the entrance and presents it to the village ruler. 'I'll light it once I'm close to the stores.'

'Thank you.' Vaja's voice is thick with emotion.

'Bah, go before you start crying and make me regret my decision.' He shoves his chief away with meaning. 'Go. Get the people to safety.'

Inside the stable, the horses are thrashing against their enclosures as they try to break free, but the doors to their stalls are too strong. The six stablemates strike the noble animals down with their long spears; the weapons are pushed deep, piercing lung and heart, releasing fountains of blood from the nostrils. The horses rear up on their hind legs to defend themselves, but it is to avail and eventually they collapse. Too weak to support their own weight any longer they gurgle and splutter with the final exhale.

The overpowering coppery stench of fresh blood mixed in with piss and manure fills the air.

Even though the young males are heartbroken, they understand the reason why it had to be done, and that reason turns their heartache into pure hatred when they see the trolls who have been left to guard the escape tunnel. The stablemates charge the small contingent of archers, running them through and killing them before they are able to call for help or even get their swords out.

Vaja makes it to the tunnel, stepping over the corpses of the invaders. 'Well met, lads. Go secure the mouth, make sure there are no more unwelcome guests waiting for us on the lower slopes.'

The six young males do as they're told without question, their desire to spill troll blood reaching lustful levels. Isfael is the next person to enter the tunnel, followed by the injured on the litters. Harlon nods at the leader of the village and runs off towards the food stores, making sure to stick to the shadows.

'I'm the last person out, Chief,' says Yelqen as he draws near to his leader.

'Very good.' Vaja takes a burning log from a nearby brazier and lobs it onto the roof of the stable. 'We'll be back. We'll reclaim and rebuild, making everything better than before.'

Although they have been pushed far beyond the limits of their physical abilities and lost several of their number, the rear guard continues to put up a valiant fight. Ghun manages to get the tip of his spear through an eye slit, making the troll to his front scream out pain. Flickering light on the far side of the village indicates that the food stores have been set alight.

A sword comes over the shields and cleaves Cathe's back open, which forces her to drop her guard and take a sword to the neck. Beaux is filled with rage as his wife drops dead by his feet. He vents his anger on the one who had slain her, but the bronze helmet robs him of his revenge.

'We can't hold them any longer,' Ghun desperately exclaims. He is struggling to thrust it at the enemy's legs as his spear seems to weigh as much as a grave marker.

Huwen is stabbed through the upper arm, yet he somehow keeps his shield up. 'Nammu's tits! We must fall back to the hut!'

After having taken a fist to the face Beaux retaliates by thrusting his spear at the one who struck him, once again failing to do much due to the thick bronze armour. 'You son of a gut parasite!'

'Withdraw! Back to the hut!' Forced to abandon their fallen the elves shuffle back under the command of Ghun who dictates the pace.

After what feels like an eternity they make it back to the long-hut and enter through the collapsed wall which is quickly barricaded up with chairs and tables.

Beaux grabs a stool and flings it at the opposite wall, giving vent to loss. 'Troll whores! I'll carve them up for killing my wife!'

'Old friend, stop that. Use that anger on the enemy.' Ghun is quick to try and calm the other male.

Beaux glares at their interim leader, his eyes are alive with the fires of hatred. 'Go chew on wolf shit, that is all I'm going to say to you.'

'What's our next move?' The sudden voice makes all of them spin around to face the speaker, yet they calm down when they see it to be Harlon stepping through a window in the south wall.

Ghun leaves the enraged Beaux to his misery. 'We go out through the front door and lure the trolls to the mine entrance.'

'You mean to get off the mountain through the mine? That's a long way to go.' Harlon remarks.

'We barricade ourselves in there. Stack the wood high and light it on fire.'

Harlon smiles. 'You want them to think we're trapped in there and committing suicide. Clever.'

'I don't rightly give a shit what they think.'

'He means to collapse the entrance by heating the rocks and making them brittle,' Beaux hisses at his fellows. 'I want to go out there and kill them, want to push my spear through their flesh and piss on their corpses.'

'Or rather come with us. Live to fight another day, have your revenge on them then.' Ghun holds his hand out in a friendly gesture. 'Come, you know the mines better than any of us. Lead us out so that we may go and warn the other elven villages that the trolls are on the warpath.'

Beaux closes his eyes and tries to force his rage to subside so that he may think more clearly. 'Very well. Let's set this new plan into motion.'

'Good to have you with us.' Ghun scoops some mead out of a clay cauldron and downs it. 'Have it up, lads and lasses. Who knows how long it'll be before we eat and drink again.'

The trolls are hacking away at the mass of tables and chairs that prevent them from getting into the house; they can't seem to remove the obstruction as everything appears to be stuck on something else. Their group bosses keep screaming orders, but the words of encouragement don't help them to gain entry into the building. Others try their best to break the back door down, yet they too find the elven building to be incredibly well constructed.

Boen is pacing around at the back of his brawlers; he knows they are tired and he wants to call an end to hostility, but the stubborn locals make that impossible, so for now the best he can do is to rotate his fighters out, allowing them a few moments to rest before ordering them back into the fray.

'Movement by the main door!' an archer screams as loud as he can before losing his arrows at the figures that are running across the courtyard.

'Dammit!' Boen can see exactly where they are heading. 'Brawlers to me! Quick!'

The trolls run after the elves, but they are weighted down by their equipment while their muscles burn with the fires of fatigue.

'Get it open!' Boen shouts and runs at the entrance, barging into the solid oak door as it is slammed shut. All he manages to do, however, is to hurt his shoulder.

The fighters around him press up against the barricade and try to push it open, but it is to no avail.

'Dammit.' Boen hits the solid wooden obstruction with the

pommel of his sword. 'Where is that wizard with his magic!?'

Gabba runs up to the mine entrance and rummages through his bag to get at the small clay pots. 'I'm here! Get your fighters back, this stuff will eat the meat off their bones.'

'Just open the doors!'

Giddy with anticipation the wizard lobs the pots at the entrance. The moments go by, yet the doors show no signs of crumbling to dust.

'I... what?' Gabba approaches the entry to the mine and uses his sword to poke at the obstruction. 'Is this pitch stopping my magic?'

Boen orders his fighters to find axes. 'Get out of the way, your magic has done nothing to help us.'

'It's them – the elves have a way of making it useless!'

'Take your excuses and shove them up your arse,' swears Boen as he points at the large house where the elven rulers live. 'Go and see if they've left anything useful in there.'

Gabba snorts loudly to dislodge a glob of phlegm from the back of his throat and then walks off, mumbling to himself that it is not his fault the magic has failed.

'Slippery little eels, these elves,' comments Rool who has joined the leader of the brawlers.

'Indeed they are.'

He smiles at the other boss. 'Is that admiration I hear in your voice?'

'It is.' Boen takes his helmet off and sits down on an overturned wheelbarrow. 'We had the upper hand; we came here under the cloak of surprise and night and yet they outsmarted us. Outfought us and caused many casualties amongst our ranks.'

Smoke begins to rise out of the mine entrance.

'What in the name of Fonolite's balls is the meaning of that?' The cuss words roll off the scout boss's tongue with incredible ease.

'Have they committed suicide in there?' Boen gets to his feet again.

'I couldn't tell you.'

'Water, we need water!' Boen roars at the infiltrators who are watching the flames grow.

Rool follows suit and screams at the fighters directly under his command. 'Don't just stand there! Get water! Douse that fire, you inbred sods!'

Hearing their superior have a go at them gets the infiltrators moving.

The scout boss pulls another wheelbarrow closer and sits down, he is smiling from ear to ear. 'We should let them burn.'

'You do realise that they are trying to collapse the entrance?'

'Let them. The town is ours, we can dig it out once our people are settled here.'

Boen sits back down again. 'Perhaps we should let the fighters rest. They've had a hard time of it.'

'Perhaps.' Rool watches his infiltrators and scouts chuck buckets of water on the blazing fire. 'Leave it, lads! It's too late now!'

Realising that there is no point in fighting the flames, they drop the buckets and just stand there, enjoying the warmth.

Rool looks at his fellow commander. 'Have you ever eaten elf before? Their meat is incredibly tender.'

'I do not want to know the tale behind that statement.'

The scout boss responds with a malicious grin.

FLEEING

It is still dark when the people of Bravin stumble onto the rock strewn bank of the Liyko River. Behind them lies a narrow strip of trees that grow along the base of the mountain, and on the ground is a thin blanket of white as the snows have arrived early this year.

'Don't stop.' Vaja urges his people to keep moving. 'We have to get to Leccy Bridge, come.'

'Just a little rest, please, Chief,' one of the younger elves who used to work the mine begs.

'No, we must keep moving, if only at slow pace. Once you stop, you have to work much harder to start again. Now come on.'

Yelqen drags the young male to his feet. 'Get up and stop feeling sorry for yourself.'

Several people look to the young wych, perhaps she can use the injured as leverage to convince the chief to let them rest for a bit, but they are out of luck. 'We're not dressed to be out here in this weather. None of us have warm clothes at hand to guard against the cold. We stop now, we all perish.'

'But the injured must be cared for, not true?' The complaint comes from Meeka, the chief's eldest daughter.

Saari slaps her child behind the head. 'Stop your moaning.'

Isfael waves the question off. 'I can check on the injured while we move, not much else I can do as there is no light and no roof over my head to keep them warm and safe. We must keep moving.'

'You heard the chief and the healer. Keep moving or I'll stick a spear in you and leave you here for the bears and wolves.' The threat comes from Menim who is clearly not in the mood for anyone's complaints. 'Our elders have stayed behind to buy us our freedom, buy it with their lives, their blood. Do not make a mockery of their sacrifice. Now get going.'

Yelqen pulls the enraged male to one side and whispers: 'Appreciate your vigour, my friend, but we must keep a front of cohesion. We can't let our masks slip like that.'

It takes a moment for the words to sink in, but eventually Menim gets the message. 'You're right, I understand. Apologies.'

'No need to apologise. Go, get to the front. I'll bring up the rear.'

'By the spirit of Nammu, my legs are spent.' Arcim is breathing heavily; beside him is his husband, Seif, who is trying to catch his breath.

'You doing well there, Seif?' Yelqen tries to encourage the village steward.

'No. I'm not. Life up there on the molehill has made me unwell. I've not run like this since I was a youngster.' He clutches his chest. 'Nammu be damned, it hurts.'

Arcim's eyes grow large with concern. 'Seif, my love, is your heart failing you?'

The other male drops to his knees. 'I don't know... I just know it hurts.'

Yelqen sprints off to go in search of his wife.

When Isfael finds the steward lying on his back heaving she quickly says a chant to awaken her healer's sight. 'Let's have a look at you.' She can see his heart beating away rapidly, but apart from that there is not much else of note. 'I don't think you're having a failing heart, but you might have put too much strain on it in a very short span of time. You need to keep moving, and we must adjust the pace to fit your abilities.'

'You certain he won't die of the Bravin curse?' Arcim is almost hysterical.

'No, his heart doesn't show the same signs as those who have succumbed to it,' replies Isfael while she helps the male to his feet. 'I'll have another look once we are somewhere warm and he has calmed down. It's difficult to see anything when the heart is thumping away so fast. I'll ask the chief to slow the pace.'

Moving towards Leccy bridge is difficult as most of the riverbank is littered with large smooth stones and boulders that make it impossible to travel in a straight line while the pebbles are woefully unstable underfoot and give way when tread upon. The litter bearers struggle more than anyone else as they are continually stumbling on the loose surface; the increased effort eats into their strength and leads to constant stopping that makes the going much harder. One of the litter bearers collapses due to over-excursion, forcing Isfael to take up his corner while simultaneously trying to drag him along, but she is overloaded and unable to move.

Several males come to her aid, forcing the healer to relinquish her spot and to let go of the exhausted male who carried the litter all the way down the scree slope. Deima is pulled back to his feet by his friends who support most of his weight between them.

Isfael leans up against a boulder, trying to regain her bearings as the world closes in on her. Someone takes hold of her elbow and helps her to get moving again, despite the exhaustion. As she notices that the hand which is guiding her feels cold, stiff and clammy, she turns her head to see who this person might be: The rotting features of an elf-like face glare at her with missing eyes and a slack jaw.

She screams out in shock, staggering back and stumbling over the rocks in an attempt to get away. The decaying figure goes after her, its bony hands reaching for her, an incoherent moan rolling out of its throat. Other dead things walk out of the water and the tree line, their hollow eye sockets fixed on the young wytch. The light snowfall turns into a drizzle of blood while the river becomes red. All along the shoreline, the trees burst into flames; it is a cold fire that steals away the warmth. Isfael finds herself with her back against a boulder, unable to escape the encroaching corpses bearing down on her.

They crowd her and claw at her clothes, her skin, her soul, causing the wytch to scream.

'Isfael!'

In an instant the world of blood and corpses melts away and she finds herself cradled in the arms of her husband; relieved to be held so close, she hugs him with all her might. 'Thank Mother Nammu for you.'

'Isfael, what is the matter?' Yelqen is deeply concerned.

'I just had a… a vision of sorts,' she replies in a low, fearful voice.

Most of the other villagers stand around, gawping at the healer, but it is hard to make out their expression in the dark.

Yelqen helps her to her feet. 'A vision? Must've been one scary moment because I've never heard you scream like that.'

'It was horrible, so horrible.'

'You see!? She now has visions! The young wytch is showing a fourth talent!' Rhonda is quick to pounce.

'Oh give it a rest, you old bag,' Yelqen shoots the wytch superior down. 'We've enough to worry about without you throwing more into the mix.'

'She is beguiling you all! She will be the undoing of the Bravin clan!'

Vaja drags the elderly female off to one side where he shares a few choice words in an attempt to try and get her to understand that there are much more pressing matters at hand.

Isfael, who ignores the ramblings of her former tutor, smiles at her husband. 'Thank you for being there for me.'

'Any time. But you must discuss this with me once we're safe.'

She nods at the request. 'I will.'

Yelqen kisses her and makes his way to the back of the column again so that he may provide a rear guard. As she pulls the sleeve of her dress back the imprint of a hand is revealed that causes a similar sensation as sunburn. Isfael grimaces when she slides her sleeve down to cover it up.

Vaja stops and waits for the rest of the column to catch up to him. He is looking around but finds it difficult to see the line of people behind him as there is little ambient light and none of them have brought any torches. He helps his wife climb over a shingle of rocks and branches that were deposited by last winter's floods. 'We should rethink this path – our escape, I mean – once we have the village back.'

'Or we can just live below the mountain like everyone else. The good folk of Tin do not live right next to their mines. Why do we?' There is a hint or irritability in Saari's tone.

The chief frowns at her. 'I suspect there to be something pressing on your mind.'

'There is,' says the chieftess as she helps a young mother and her babe get over the shingle. 'But we shall converse once we have a moment to ourselves.'

Vaja contemplates her reply before heading to the front of the column again.

When the sun begins to rise in the east the Bravin clan nears Leccy Bridge. Those standing watch by the river crossing can see the gaggle of people approaching them and send word to their leader to inform him of a large group that is heading towards their position.

An elf by the name of Mounra steps out of his lodgings and hurries up the road so that he may hear what the newcomers might have to say. 'Greetings! What brings you down the mountain?'

Vaja holds his spear over his head. 'Greetings. We've come to seek refuge.'

'Refuge from what?' Mounra is resting his hand on the pommel of his sword, ready to strike should the other elf give him any reason.

'Trolls.' Out of breath, Vaja keeps his response short.

'Your village was set on by trolls? This news does not hold a bright outcome for us.' Mounra gestures at several of his subordinates. 'Lead them in, then report to the chief that they have suffered the same fate as Tin.'

'Tin has also been taken?' Vaja's croaks because he is so thirsty.

Mourna pulls his mouth into a thin line and gives a slight nod. 'Indeed they have.' He then moves closer to the village leader and places a reassuring hand on his shoulder. 'You and your people are among friends now.'

'It is good to know kindness in a time of need,' the chief speaks and gives a slight bow to show his respect before leading his people across the bridge.

A rock tumbles down the northern scree slope. Ghun, who watches it go, asks: 'How long do you think we spent in the mine?'

Beaux squints as he steps out of the small cave opening and into the bright morning. 'All night, I'd say.'

'How are you feeling, old friend?'

Beaux shakes his head: before he replies: 'Like going back up there and having a fight with those horse apples.'

'I feel your anger...'

'You have no idea about my anger.' Beaux waves the other male off. 'Now go, get the warning out. I've done my part, led you through the mines.'

'And now you can go back to Selkie, back to your original village, warn them of the trolls and their desires to control all the land.'

'We don't have to warn anyone of anything,' Harlon chimes in. He is squatting close to the mouth of the cave, lingering there to allow his eyes to adjust to the changing light. 'The trolls are after our copper, just as the chief said.'

'Perhaps they want Selkie too, and Kelpie. Who knows how far their ambitions stretch?' Ghun counters.

'They would've sailed right past Kelpie on the Liyko River where it crosses the grasslands. I'm sure they would've sacked that village already.' Harlon points out an obvious fact. 'We should just go round the Grand Peak, make our way to Keties.'

'No, Ghun is right.' Beaux sides with their interim leader. 'You lot should go and warn the other villages. I need to get back up there, retrieve my wife's body and return her to Mother Nammu's embrace.'

Ghun gives his friend's shoulder a slight squeeze. 'Worry not, our dead will find their way back to the arms of our goddess.'

Annoyed at being ignored, Harlon raises his voice: 'Do any of you even listen to me? Have you heard what I've said about Kelpie?'

'They wouldn't have sacked the horse riders. There's no way they could take on such a large village with the number that attacked us, and win. If a greater force would've done so, then we would've gotten wind of it.' Beaux sounds sure of himself. 'I'll suspect that we were the first to be taken on. An army on the move securing raw materials for itself. We do as Ghun has said, we split up and go warn the others.'

'What do you think the future holds for Tin?' The random question comes from an old male named Croesig who is nursing a cut to his forearm.

'We'll learn that later,' Ghun responds and picks his spear up. 'Are we committing to this task or are we just going to cluster together like little fish and warble our way round the mountain?'

All of them agree that getting a warning out to the other villages is the best use of their strength, so they split up into two groups, say their final farewells and set off.

DELIBERATIONS

The chief of Keties stands by the gate which connects the trade quarter with the living quarter, observing the hustle and bustle. Beside him is his wife who sketches out what she sees with charcoal on a vellum sheet. Due to its sheer size the village has been segmented into three quarters and each one given a distinct purpose; the trader quarter now houses the displaced people from the neighbouring villages.

Locals are hard at work to accommodate their fellow elves, to ease the burdens that have been thrust upon them. People use whatever they are given or have scavenged to try and build some sort of shelter for themselves and their loved ones. Desperation is written on the faces of all, and fear makes them work harder than they've ever worked in their lives.

Benue's dark skin, tightly curled hair, broad nose and thick lips are clear indications that he originates from the lands to the south, just like the chieftess. He pulls his cloak up to keep the cold wind out of his neck and then turns to speak with the second wytch superior of Keties. 'Farnu, can you summon the chiefs, chieftesses and their wytches to our hut? Tell them to bring their metalworkers and bowyers along. We need to discuss this matter without delay.'

She gives a slight bow. 'Certainly.'

'Thank you.'

Selves, the chieftess of Keties, gestures at the five large stone towers that occupy the middle of the living quarter. 'Can you also place guards by the doors of the brochs and give them explicit orders to whip anyone who tries to get in without a Steward's Seal. We don't want the hungry to get any ideas.'

The second wytch seems taken aback by the command.

Benue looks over to the food stores. 'My wife has a point there.'

'I will get it done.' Farnu makes a mental note of her orders and sets off to go and fulfil her duty.

Dressed in a simple one-piece tunic that was gifted to her by the villagers who took them in Isfael is the last to arrive at the summons. She bows to show her respect. 'I apologise for my tardiness and my appearance. My hostess was beset by birthing cramps early this morning and the child arrived in the world not too long ago.'

Benue stands and returns the gesture. 'No need to apologise. It is folks as yourself who keep us healthy and alive. The stains on your clothes and your hands pay testament to your importance. I thank you for your service, I thank all wytches.' He pivots on the spot to give a bow to each healer present at the meeting.

All of the wytches in the gathering get up and return the gesture of respect.

'Right, now that we're done pushing hails and praises up the arseholes of all herb collectors in the hut, can we get to the point of this get-together?' Safair, chief of Tin, blurts, his fingers tracing the two thick purple scars on the side of his head.

Benue forces a smile; he knows that the other chief's mind has been compromised by a head injury he suffered a few years back. 'Certainly.' He taps the shoulder of one of the record keepers sat by his feet. 'The six of you start your notes now.' Next his gaze returns to the other village leaders. 'We need to discuss the manner in which the trolls have bested your defences and adjust ours accordingly.'

'Pah, they won't set foot on this spit of land. There's nothing of value to be had here.' Safair immediately dismisses the worries of his equal.

Vaja rolls his eyes and decides to start things off. 'They wore thick metal plate on their chests and helms made of the same material on their heads. Their heavy shields also offer protection from our spears, and the square shape seems to help them lock together much better, but that also means they have to move as a unit, they can't be as fluid as we are with our round shields.' He clears his throat. 'One shortcoming we noted in their garb was their legs and feet. We managed to get the upper hand by stabbing them low.'

'So we can be sure that they would've addressed that problem by the time they come to face us.' Benue nods. 'Thanks for that observation. Anything else?'

'Wait a count or two.' Safair gets to his feet and points at the chief sitting across the hearth. 'How did you manage to get into a fighting formation? We were still celebrating the onset of winter when those buggers stormed in and laid waste to us.' His voice is filled with sorrow, making it sound as if he is about to cry. 'How is it that you managed to get most of your people out while mine died!?'

Saari shuffles to the edge of her seat. 'We have a hunter who possesses the talent of outreach. He sensed the trolls the moment they entered our village, allowing us to get our spears up.'

Safair draws his finger back and buries his fist under his robes. 'How is it that we didn't have talent among our people? Why does Nammu not love us as much?'

Feila, the chieftess of Tin, gets up and hugs her husband, making sure to bury his face in her shoulder while she speaks with the chief of Keties. 'Only a small part of their fighters wore the plates and helms. The rest are archers or lightly dressed fighters – but make no mistake, they're very well trained in the art of sword play.'

Isfael stands up and takes an item out of her bag. 'They use metal-tipped missiles with barbs that are swept back very aggressively, which makes the arrow hold fast in the wound. I suspect that heads of these missiles are not sharpened properly and I think it is done to prevent them punching through... let's say an arm or a leg when struck. I think the trolls do this to incapacitate, not kill.'

'So their aim is to injure those they face.' Benue thinks for a second. 'Yes, that makes sense. Fighters will step on the dead, but an injured mate laying on the ground could be a hindrance. A wounded fighter will also take up resources once dragged off the line.' He shakes his head before he continues: 'These trolls are nasty buggers.'

'Can I please see that arrowhead?' Meyla, the first wytch superior of Keties, gestures for the other healer to come closer.

Isfael obliges and moves around the hearth. 'See the backwards-facing barbs?'

'The wound from that will be unpleasant to say the least.' Meyla takes the item and presses it against his palm. 'How do you remove this? Do you just cut it out like an abscess?'

Isfael shakes her head while pulling a couple of goose feathers out of her bag. 'With the Chief's approval, I'll show how I did it.'

Benue gets up and approaches the healers. 'This I want to see.'

The Bravin wytch explains: 'Cut the feathers off, you don't need those. Remove the pointy end of the shaft. That leaves you with the hollow bits of the quill, like two short straws. Let your ward know that it will hurt before you push your little finger into the wound. Locate the barbs, then very gently flatten each quill so that it can go in and follow the path of the cut that the arrow has made. Push the shafts over each barb as this will prevent them from catching flesh on the way out as you withdraw it. We can practice on some dead swine after the deliberations if the Chief would allow that.'

Benue looks at her with appreciation. 'Well done. You have my permission to shoot up some pigs for the benefit of learning this technique.'

'And you came up with this method when the trolls were ransacking your village?' Feilah is astounded by what she hears. 'Our wytches just broke the arrows off and bandaged the injury to try and stop the head from moving too much and digging in deeper.'

Isfael gives a slight shrug. 'I had to think fast as that first wave of arrows had left quite a few of our people injured.'

'On the subject of their bows, I've had a look at one.' Fauk stands up, his left arm in a sling because a troll stabbed him in the shoulder during the initial brawl. 'Their method of bow making is old, one that was familiar to my grandfather. The design is simple but effective. Their weapons are carved out of yew and the strings are made from hemp string instead of sinew.'

'If it's so great then why don't we use it?!' Once again it is Safair who barks the question out.

Fauk decides to humour the chief. 'Our peoples have been hunting the thick forest of this land for a very long time now. The long wood stave bows of yesteryear turned out to be too cumbersome in the thickets, so we came up with layer horn bows. Smaller in size but packing the same punch.'

Benue glares at the leader of Tin while addressing the whole gathering. 'To come back to the trolls, they give heavy protection to a small number of what I can only surmise to be their best fighters. Could we clad our own fighters in a similar fashion?'

The metalworker from Keties stands up, joined by the one native to Tin. 'We've listened to the people describe the plate to us and we must admit, Chief, it will take a lot of raw materials to make such armour. Neither of us are sure that we possess the skills or the workforce to craft the plates any time soon. It'll take months of trial and error to replicate the achievements of the trolls.'

'Thank you, Hucken, for your candour.' Benue thinks for a moment. 'We'll need raw materials anyway, regardless of whether we try to replicate the inventions of the enemy or not. We're short on swords and spears. We can definitely use their arrowhead designs against them. To get more metal, I'd suggest sending divers into the river at the south end of the eyot, by the old Sedie tree. Have them retrieve the offerings we laid there to appease Leau.'

It is a suggestion that makes the first wytch superior of Keties choke on his own tongue, causing him to jump out of his chair. 'Pardon!? You want us to take back what we've given to the river goddess in good faith?'

The chief sits back in his chair. 'It's a matter of life and death, Meyla. I'm sure she'll understand.'

'I must protest this decision.'

Benue gets up and approaches the first wytch, his demeanour is one of understanding. 'I shall note your protest, but I hold firm that we must retrieve all the metalwork we've seeded to Leau, because we are short on choices here.'

Meyla sits back down, his face pale with worry.

'I'll do my best to win favour with the river goddess,' Selves, the chieftess of Keties, offers.

Benue gives her a bow. 'Thank you, my love. The gods have a soft spot for you.'

'Pfft,' Safair mocks, 'we don't have to worry. It's already started to snow. No one fights in deep snow.'

Vaja balls his fist up to control his anger. 'I must disagree with you there, old friend. My village was covered in snow up to half-shin deep. It didn't stop them then. The trolls came at us like they were driven by hate and they didn't stop. Make no mistake, they will come here and they will drive us off this island too if we don't get ourselves organised.'

'I say horseshit to your claim,' Safair spits as he extends to his full height. 'Besides, your grandfather was the one stupid enough to build a village at the top of a mountain. Your grandfather, not mine! So stop your crying.'

Everyone in the gathering looks around, evidently confused by the remark.

Benue takes it upon himself to dispel the ill feeling that has suddenly permeated the air. 'Right. We'll reclaim both Tin and Bravin, but first we must secure the eyot.'

Safair faces the other chief, slamming his hands onto his hips; the motion causes his cloak to fly open and reveal the thick purple scars that cover most of his pigeon chest. 'What!? Why!?

There is nothing here of value! We must simply walk over there and get Tin back from those soulless demons!'

'I beg to differ, my good fellow.' Benue remains calm. 'We have some of the best farmland around, a never-ending supply of water and the ground doesn't freeze in winter. The Liyoko River keeps us warm throughout the cold months.'

'My village gives you the soft silver you crave for your metalworks! We give you the sands to make your metals better! Tin is an important village.'

Benue gives his equal a warm smile. 'Yes, Tin is an important village and we will get it back.'

When Feilah gets to her feet and whispers something in her husband's ear, he nods a few times and sits back down, chewing on his thumb. 'I apologise, Chief of Keties, for my outburst. I'm not feeling myself today.'

Benue bows before he replies: 'No need to apologise. All of us are upset by this new development.' He faces the others. 'Now, what have we got in terms of strategy to keep the enemy on the other side of the river until we're ready to attack?'

The militia chief, who is carrying a thick ledger with a proposal inside it, steps forward and hands the document over to his chief while beginning to explain how they could go about shoring up their defence.

Saari leans over to her husband and whispers: 'Where is our so-called wytch superior?'

'She said she didn't feel well. Blamed it on the trek here.'

'You must remove her, let Isfael take up the mantle.'

'I've spoken to her on that subject before, she's stubborn.' Vaja finds it impossible to keep the tint of irritation out of his voice.

The chief of Keties shoots them a poisonous stare. 'Any other ideas I can consider?'

Vaja shakes his head. 'No, nothing that I can add at this moment.'

'Very good. Then I call the morning deliberations to a close.' Benue gesture for everyone to get up and leave. 'Now go, fill your bellies. We shall gather again once we've eaten.'

The rulers of Bravin are on their way back to the small hut that they and their children have been allocated when the wytch superior stops them.

'How nice of you to finally make an appearance.' Saari can't hide her disdain for the elderly female.

Vaja picks up on her tone. 'May I speak with the superior in private, please?'

Saari gives a slight bow of the head. 'Certainly.'

'Thank you, my love,' says Vaja and leads the old healer into a nearby barn; it is mostly empty as the oxen are out ploughing the fields, despite the snow. 'Why were you not at the deliberations?'

'I've been keeping an eye on that young wytch of ours.'

'Oh, for the love of our Mother's grace, can you please stop that?' Vaja's shoulders droop, giving him a slouched posture. 'Just stop.'

'No, I shall not!' She pulls something out of the bleached cloth purse tied to her belt. 'This – this thing – is filled with an evil I've never sensed before and it was amongst Isfael's stuff.'

Vaja glares at the gem and then at the one presenting it. 'You stole something of hers? Have you gone mad?'

'It's filled with foul powers. Foul!'

The chief picks the gem up and rolls it around between his fingers; he can sense the aura of discomfort that surrounds it but decides that it is not worthy of his attention. 'I do not feel it.' He shoves the stone back in the superior's hand. 'Return it or I'll have you flogged for thievery.'

'You must oust her from the clan. You must drive her away, send her into the wilderness.'

As Rhonda is wildly gesturing off into the distance, Vaja almost loses his temper. 'Enough! I'm not speaking about this anymore. Isfael is a damn good healer. She pulled a few back from the brink the other night when the trolls attacked. She managed to cure many ailments when she returned from the harvesting tour, ailments that you struggled to do anything about. In fact, I want you to step down, relinquish the role of wytch superior to her.'

'You...' Rhonda sounds close to tears. 'You want to take away my status? I've held that post longer than you've been alive, you ungrateful little shit.'

'You've had your run. Now is your time to step down and enjoy your twilight years free of responsibility and stress. My decision is final and I'll call a meeting to announce it to the rest of our clan.'

'She killed the caravan master!' Rhonda grasps at her final lifeline.

'Have you proof of this claim?'

'She grabbed hold of his hands when they quarrelled! He fled from her, ran to his house where he died of sudden heart failure.' Again Rhonda's gestures are exuberant. 'Go ask Aunah or Feilbard or Cuthes. They saw the exchange between Klouven and the young wytch. They saw!'

Vaja buries his face in his palm. 'Mother Nammu grant me strength, please.' He glares at the old healer through his fingers before lowering his hand. 'When was this?'

'Shortly after they returned from the markets.'

'That...' Vaja takes a moment to reign his anger in. 'They returned two days before the trolls attacked. Are you telling me the old caravan master was lying dead in his hut for two days, and you told no one? How did he die?'

Rhonda is struck by the selfishness of her desires but decides to double down. 'He would've been alive if not for that she-wolf.'

'How did he die?' Vaja slightly raises his voice.

'Clutched his chest, collapsed and passed away next to his hearth.'

'Were you there? Did you just stand there and watch Klouven die? Did you not ply your trade?'

As soon as Rhonda realises that she is being pushed into a corner she goes silent.

'Answer me, right now!'

'I saw it...'

Vaja closes in on the elderly female. 'You saw it through the eyes of some animal, didn't you? You employed your talent to drop in on Klouven, watched him die a miserable death, and now you are here trying to use that underhanded method of yours to win favours.' He takes a step back. 'You're now officially an old wytch. Starting this very moment you're no longer allowed to practise healing magic.'

Rhonda's demeanour changes instantly; gone is the sorrowful old female, replaced by a bitter one that spits on the ground, flinging the gem into a pile of muck. 'You ungrateful shit! I pulled you out of your mother's birth passage. I brought you into this world. I helped you survive the fever that decimated our village, the fever that took your father. I'm the Wytch Superior of Bravin and now you want to put some Selkie she-dog in my place? You and everyone who supports that gut parasite will suffer the wrath of the gods!'

'You arrogant old sow! Now I see my mistake. I should've removed you from your post long ago. But I've kept you there, thinking I was showing you respect. Worst of all, your incompetence cost someone their life and yet you want to make it out to be my fault? Or the fault of another wytch? You have become a despicable beast. You are the gut parasite, not Isfael.'

She waves him off and scurries away. 'Go romance a horse, stupid whelp!'

The chief wants to go after her but is stopped by the sudden appearance of the young wytch who steps in front of him and places a gentle hand on his chest.

Isfael seems to glow in the pale autumn sun, her eyes locked on her former tutor as she storms off. 'Age affects the mind. I remember many of the older folks in Selkie turning nasty in their later years, seemingly unable to accept that they are getting older. Or perhaps the mind begins to wear thin with the passage of the years – all those thoughts and emotions, they must take a toll.' She folds her arms. 'It's a terrible thing to see such great souls turn bitter as time claims them bit by bit and knowing there is nothing we can do to stop it.'

Vaja leans up against the door frame, looking off towards the gate that connects the market sector with the living quarters. 'How much of that did you hear?'

'Most of it. I'm sorry, I didn't mean to eavesdrop, but I heard my name mentioned on the way past.' Isfael notices the gem in the pile of dung and walks over to retrieve it. 'You haven't seen my husband perchance?' she asks as she watches the animal faeces glide off its smooth surface, grimacing at its sting. 'I had hoped that this thing would be lost up there on the mountain but that was my mistake.'

'I apologise for Rhonda's theft. And no, I've not seen your husband.'

'No need to be sorry for what she did. And please, don't have her flogged. She's just afraid of losing everything she has worked so hard for in her life. She offered up a lot, forgoing a family to be the best wytch she could be. Despite her actions Rhonda deserves our admiration, not our scorn.'

Vaja frowns at the mention of a flogging. 'It was an empty threat. But I am very angry about the fact that she watched one of our own die by the Bravin curse and failed to go to his aid. Poor Klouven, lying dead in his hut while we feasted.'

'That I can't defend. Unless the superior's mind is much further gone than I had imagined.'

'Speaking of which.' Vaja gets to his full height, faces the healer and extends his right hand, palm facing up. 'I appoint you Wytch Superior of Bravin and its folk.'

Isfael curtsies to show that she accepts the appointment. 'It will be an honour to serve you and the people of Bravin in the role of Wytch Superior.'

'We shall make it official tomorrow evening if circumstances permit. Until then I ask that you keep this between us.' Vaja steps closer to her and whispers: 'Before we part ways, why did you tint my wife's drink with that mind-melting mix of herbs and roots?'

Isfael shakes her head. 'No, please don't ask me. You and Saari will have to talk about that; it's not for me to comment on. I just aided her with medicines concerning her needs.'

The chief huffs. 'Right then. See you at this evening's deliberations.'

Isfael walks away from the barn and slips into a small passage between two huts where she lets out the grunt of pain that she's been suppressing ever since she retrieved the gem from the muck. 'Damndible thing! I should just throw it in the river.'

'Her... saver... life...' The words surge through her mind, almost bringing her to her knees.

'Gah!' Isfael drops the gem and grabs the sides of her head. 'What are you?'

'Her... saver... life...' The sounds of battle are mixed in with the raspy voice that seems to be taking on a more menacing tone with each word.

She grabs the gem off the ground and shoves it in her purse. 'I can't leave you laying around.'

'You... saver... life... saver... to us.' The tone changes again, sounding more desperate.

'Dammit. Stop it. Stop it!' She squeezes the purse as hard as she can and, to her surprise, the voices and the echoes of battle cease. 'You can understand me? How can a stone be this powerful?'

'Saver of life... must save us... can save us.' This time the words carry less malice; instead they sound more like a group speaking over each other.

'You can understand me. Is there a person inside you?'

The gem remains silent.

Isfael taps the purse. 'Now that I've asked a question it stops speaking. Stupid rock.' She pulls her sleeve up to look at the handprint; it has changed from sunburn red to light tan. 'Perhaps I should go to the old wytch's hut, check their records. See what knowledge lies in those scrolls... Maybe, just maybe, I'll find something about this gem.' She throws her hands up. 'And now I'm talking to myself. What is this thing doing to me?'

Saari sits next to the small hearth and tends the fire while her daughter adds some chopped root vegetables to the stew she's been brewing for midday meal. 'Welcome… home, my love. What did the old wytch have to say for herself?'

Vaja walks over to their bedroom, gesturing for his wife to join him. 'May we speak under four eyes, please?'

She hands the ladle over to her daughter and follows him. 'Certainly.'

The chief closes the door before removing his cloak and dropping it on the pile of sleeping skins. 'Why do you consume those herbs?'

Saari gives him a sidelong glance. 'Beg your...'

'No, please. I've had to deal with the stubborn old wytch and my rope is now completely uncoiled. Just be honest with me.'

She folds her arms, her eyes never leaving those of her husband. 'I hate it up there on that mountain. I've hated it since my father married me off to you. Those herbs help me cope with the feeling of being trapped.'

'Do you hate me?'

Saari lets out a sigh. 'No, dammit. I love you with all my heart, Vaja. I willingly bore your offspring. I enjoy your company. I just hate life on top of that miserable mountain. Don't tell me the world looks wonderful and serene from up there, or something stupid like that. I've no desire to stand atop that rock and be wooed by the views. I don't see any beauty in it, I just don't.'

Vaja sits down on the clothes chest at the foot of the sleeping pile. 'Oh. Why do you hate it so much?'

'I'm an elf from the grasslands. I grew up riding across the open plains, watched the sun set and rise over the horizon, saw it colour the fields with light. I miss the rides out to Shallow Lake, I miss camping on its shores, bathing in its unblemished waters, catching the fish that swim there.'

'Right, I understand. Life before becoming chieftess was wonderful.' He scratches an eyebrow, looking up at his wife. 'Well, I can start a war with your father's tribe. Drive them off and take over his lands. Then you can do all of that again.'

Saari rolls her eyes at the immature jest.

'Or, now hear me out, we move the village to the base of the mountain. How does that sound?'

'That sounds like a wonderful idea.'

Vaja gets up and hugs his wife. 'See, I'm very clever.'

'Yes yes, you are the smartest of them all.' Saari pokes him in the side to show that she has no hard feelings.

After having kissed her on the top of her head Vaja asks: 'Why have you never spoken to me about these thing before?'

'I don't know.' Saari steps back, finding herself up against the door. 'When we met, we were both very young. Seventy-seven years old, still unsure of ourselves and stupid with inexperience. And suddenly we're married, joining two elven villages together. Then I was pregnant with Ven, and shortly after he was born, there was Esker...'

Vaja waves his hands from side to side. 'I understand. We were young, then we became parents, and I was always busy. You felt like you could never approach me.'

'Precisely.'

He puts his hands on his hips. 'I'm serious about relocating the village. The miners can stay up on the peak in the old long-hut, if it hasn't burned down. We can clear some of the forest away, have our own farms and grow our own grains and lentils.'

Saari hugs her husband again. 'Thank you.'

'We have to get Bravin back first, so don't be thanking me just yet.'

'Thank you for wanting to move a whole village for me.'

'I'd move the world for you.'

It is late in the day and the sun has already set as Benue reads the lengthy report that has just been delivered to him. Sat around the hearth are the delegation members from earlier, all of them waiting patiently. The chief thanks the hunter who brought the document and excuses him, whereupon the latter gives a bow and leaves.

Benue rubs his face and gets up so that he can walk around while thinking. 'It is clear now that Tin and Bravin were not isolated attacks. The hunting, or scouting party I should say, that I sent out this morning has located the remnants of a large troll encampment to the south, close to the Sandy Hills. Seems they have moved their camp into Tin itself, placing them not too far from our gates. Apparently the trolls have brought their entire village with them. They have come to settle these lands, that much is clear. And I suspect that we're in their way.'

Vaja stands up to speak, something that a person in his position would not normally do during such meetings. 'I must ask why they would risk a winter fight? Common sense would dictate that one must wait for the cold to dissipate before setting out on the warpath. Could we perhaps send a delegation to speak with them? Suggest a peace treaty?'

'I can only surmise that they are either stupid or desperate and thus have no other choice.' Benue points at the other chief. 'Let's hope they are stupid, because people who are desperate to survive will fight much harder than the stupid ones.'

Meyla, the first wytch superior, stands up. 'Perhaps they also want to take us on when there aren't any traders in our ports. Those would already present a significant fighting force to overcome.'

'Nah, traders will haul it back to their ships and get out while the going is good,' Vaja counters.

Isfael steps closer to the hearth to draw attention to herself. 'I've a possible explanation for their actions.'

'Go on, let's hear it.' Benue sounds slightly impatient.

'The skies have turned purple with the setting sun. I noticed it a few day back and again this day while the sun was setting. The old wytches noticed this omen before and they wrote about it. They mention famine and pestilence, forests devoid of animals to hunt and plants to scavenge. They even wrote about fields of grain failing to mature and orchards that yielded nothing. Those who were once friends would instead use the word foe.'

Benue shrugs. 'Why should we pay heed to an old tale that

was probably spoken when my great grandfather first sailed up the Liyoko River?'

'This omen could explain why they are here. Perhaps something terrible has happened in their lands. Perhaps we can discuss with them terms of peace? Offer to see them through the winter until the summer comes?' Feilah is quick to come up with a solution, based on what she has just heard.

'Peace negotiations.' Benue almost laughs at the idea. 'They made it abundantly clear that they do not wish for such a thing. I sent out two of my militia chiefs this morning to do just that. One came back carrying the head of the other.' He lowers his gaze before he continues. 'Sorry to say this, Feilah, but we are in for bloodshed and only the most aggressive clan will be victorious.'

Isfael holds her hand up to draw the attention of the chieftess across from her. 'Unfortunately, we'll be starving ourselves – it won't be possible for us to see to the food needs of others.'

'How so?' Feilah leans forward in her chair, her face appearing malicious in the glow of the hearth. 'How is it that the changing colour of the dusk sky can be so ominous?'

'The records tell of lingering winters when the purple hue can be seen in the heavens. We're backed into a corner, same as the enemies who are now stood on Keties' doorstep. All of us are trapped in a fight for survival,' Isfael coldly explains.

'Seems that we are.' Benue glares at his wytch superior, clearly annoyed that someone from a different village would be privy to the knowledge he should be holding.

'Another subject I'd like to approach, Chief, if I may.' Isfael decides to make the most of this moment. 'We do not have enough medicines for everyone, especially for those who are going to suffer wounds in the coming fight.'

'That is self-explanatory,' replies Benue and folds his arms, his eyes lingering on the Bravin healer. 'Anything you want to suggest?'

Isfael takes a deep breath. 'There's a meadow by the foot of the Sheal Mountains where the snow doesn't remain once it has fallen. Medicine plants grow there all year round, or so the ledgers claim.'

'What's the problem with this meadow? I can hear hesitation in your voice.'

'It's close to the den of a dragon.' Isfael holds her hands out to show she has not finished speaking yet. 'The records are old, so perhaps the dragon has already passed or moved on to other pastures.'

Benue unfolds his arms and walks closer to the speaker. 'The records could be out of date as you say, and this meadow might no longer exist. So, what do you suggest?'

'A small group. Two wytches, two hunters. We can set off tomorrow, before first light. It'll take us at least a day to get there and a day to get back if all goes well.'

'Keep the group light and move fast. Should it turn out to be a ghost chase, then we're not left undefended.' Benue holds his right hand out, palm facing up. 'Very well. You can select your companions. Go and get the medicines we need to see us through.'

Isfael bows. 'Thank you, Chief. I'll start my preparations immediately.' She looks over to the two wytches on the opposite side of the hearth. 'Would one of you like to join me on this venture?'

Farnu gets up. 'I'll come with you. It'll serve us well to know of this meadow's location, should it prove useful.'

Isfael bows to the chief of Keties and then faces her own village leaders. 'I'll depart, with your blessing of course.'

'Go already.' Vaja gets up and hugs her. 'Just come back in one piece. Bravin is a bit short on fixers and we still need to finalise your ascension.'

Benue doesn't wait for the wytches to leave before asking the rest of the delegation: 'Any other issues I should know about?'

Meyla gets up. 'Yes. I caught a group of youngsters defecating next to their huts earlier this day. You must instil a cleanliness law, Chief. A law we can enforce with hard labour if no one adheres to it. Otherwise we won't be able to keep the stomach upsets at bay. Once that cuts through Keties, we are done.'

Benue shakes his fists at the rafters. 'Why must we mollycoddle the people? Why can't they just be sensible?' He walks towards one of the record keepers and says: 'Make a note that all people who are caught relieving themselves within the village perimeter, without using their chamber pots, will receive twenty flogs. Children between the ages of nil years and twenty-two are excluded, as they are still nestlings under the care of their mothers.'

HERE LIVES OGLLOT

Pillars of fire reach up towards the sky. All around stand the ruins of a ransacked village, engulfed in flames. Elf-like figures clad in bone and cloth armour hack at each other, their wooden club and stone-tipped spears shining in the firelight, glistening with blood. Babes are torn from their mother's arms, their bodies broken as they are bashed against the earth. Females are thrown to the ground where they are violated before their attackers run them through in a final act of defilement.

Isfael moves to stop a warrior who is striking a young female in the face and tearing at her clothes, but touching the apparition causes the wytch to scream out in pain as images of torture flash through her mind.

'Elf.' A disembodied voice cuts through the din of battle

She gets to her knees, horrified by the dark red blood that drips from her hands. 'You haunt my dreams! You call me when I'm awake! Who are you!? What are you!? Show yourself!'

Someone or something grabs hold of her garments and tries to rip them off her body. Isfael fights back but finds that her punches carry no weight; she is powerless to stop her own violation, no matter how much she fights against her assailant.

'Yelqen!' Her cries for help seem to have no power either, her words sucked up by the air in front of her face. 'Yelqen!'

'Elf!'

A hand grabs her by the mouth and pushes her head into

the dirt; the accompanying voice drips with malice and the sour breath invades her sense of smell, filling her with a fear she has never felt before. 'Gadnav trov kei ijaan jhoe. Roëeh. Vhamparuse roëeh!'

She continues to put up a valiant struggle, but her efforts are futile; her clothes are torn off, her limbs pinned and unable to move. The weight of the dark figure bears down on her, and she can soon feel an uncomfortable pressure between her legs. She screams in defiance, desperately fighting against the hands restraining her.

Silence. Darkness.

A tiny light flickers into existence.

'Life this. Day to day.'

Isfael finds herself lying on air, her garments intact, the violation never happened. 'What was that!? Where am I!?'

'Day to day, for hundred season I see that what you did see. I see lover and daughter. I see enemy take them. I see enemy make bad of them,' speaks the voice, heavy with emotion. 'Lover and daughter of I. Them I see get made dirty by enemy, see this for hundred seasons.'

She tries to sit up, but there is nothing to push against. 'Who are you!? What do you want!?'

'Hundred seasons...'

'Yes, I get it! I understand,' Isfael yells in distress. 'I get it! You... you've been reliving the horrors of watching your wife and your daughter get defiled by your enemies, I take it, and it's been ongoing for a hundred seasons now. Why put me through that!? Why make me feel those things!?'

'Elf.' The flickering light moves closer; it appears to be a firefly cradled in the hands of a warrior who is clad in bone armour. 'Elf must to know.'

'I must know what!? Why must I know that!? What purpose does this serve!?' She screams at the person shrouded in darkness. 'Must I know what it feels like to be at the mercy of someone who hates me!?'

The warrior helps her to gain her orientation, his touch ever so gentle. 'Elf to know, me not make elf see. Jewel make elf see that. Me take elf back from seeing the bad, from feeling the bad.'

'You pulled me away from that horrible experience?' Her tone drops to a whisper. 'Or are you toying with me?'

'Not must any feel dat. Not must any live that.' He moves the light around without really touching it and shows off his calloused palms. 'Strong is hands of I. Strong, but not can I to keep safe lover of I and daughter of I. Them is find in field, by I. Warm was day. World of green. No water come from sky. Not seen is cloud.' There is a long pause filled with the sputtering of a person suppressing their tears. 'War I fight, war I win. All I lost.'

Isfael's heart breaks at hearing the defeat in his voice and reaches out to cradle the elf-like face in her hands. 'Why do you call me here in my sleep? What is it you want of me?'

The figure's voice turns hard and dark. 'Power you is feel. Person of skill is you. You is good. Save Burbur.'

'Your name is Burbur?'

'Burbur is all. Burbur is I and oder to be here in jewel.'

Isfael thinks before she asks: 'Burbur, you part of a group? Are there many of you in there, in this gem?'

'Burbur is many of I.'

'It's time to wake up. We've to leave soon.'

Isfael looks around, confused. 'Yelqen?'

'Come, get up. Your tour waits for you.' The whispering voice drifts down out of nowhere.

Isfael looks back at the one she has been speaking with. 'Wait. What is your name!?'

'Ogllot.'

'What do you want of me!?'

'Ogllot and Ischeel later to speak.'

WORTH

A troll delegation is making its way to the long-hut of Tin where they are awaited by their king who has laid claim to the building and renamed it the King's House. The entire troll army has taken up residence in the village, their bosses and wizards having taken all of the round huts, while the fighters have been left to their own devices. They have, however, proven their adaptability and managed to build small shelters for themselves and their families, using what raw materials they could source in the surrounding forests.

Most of the trolls are spellbound by the land surrounding them; never before have they seen so many trees nor so much arable soil.

Teshu is looking at the creation before him. The first thing he did when he walked into Tin was to order his servants to cover up the hearth so that his artist could make a sand table. Next he ordered the artist to sculpt an accurate representation of the elven village that is located on the eyot a mere twelve miles away. They have assured him that the details are correct in all respects, save for the scale. He has taken them on their word, for if they fail him, they'll be whipped until they die of blood loss or shock.

Light is provided by oil lamps and their reflective copper back plates, all of which are suspended from the rafters. The delegation moves round so that they can get a clear view of the representation, each giving a cursory bow as they pass the king. All are clad in dark linen robes and have silver plates draped around their necks to depict which role they play in court. The king is the only one present who is wearing a white linen tunic and dress with a red belt that holds his short sword on his left hip; a pair of woven grass slippers keep the worst of the cold at bay.

'We're shoring up our holdouts by the bridgeheads that lead off the island.' The strategies wizard uses a reed to indicate the twigs that represent the river crossings. 'If they try to leave by those means, we'll be able to drive them back.'

'What about river crossings conducted by boats or dugouts?' Teshu enquires.

'We've got archery outposts positioned in the trees along the riverbank to be on the lookout for just such attempts.'

Teshu's facial expression indicates that he is not convinced. 'Best you have a few patrols move around in the gaps between the outposts. We wouldn't want the elves to supplement their food stores. It'd be best to face them if they are slightly underfed. Starving would be preferable, but we are short on time so the first will have to do for us.'

'I'll do better, my King.'

'See that you do.' Teshu studies the model. 'So, tall wooden palisades around the entire town, with defensive ditches in front of and behind each one. Three rows deep. The approach is angled, of course, forcing any attacker to remain within the killing plot for much longer, compared to a straight through approach. Clever.' His eye is drawn to the interior layout. 'Each sector is cordoned off by a palisade wall of its own. Luckily no ditches there, but still a formidable defence when all your fighters are tired.' He points at the five smooth stones that have been planted in the heart of the living quarter. 'What are those? Towers for archers?'

The wizard of intellect steps forward. 'No, my King. To the best of our knowledge, those are food stores. Considering their size, they'll be very valuable to us once we've taken the town.'

'If they don't set fire to them first.' Teshu rubs his chin. 'Best to assume they will put archers on those things, nice vantage point. Actually, you won't even need archers, children with large stones can also do a lot of damage from up there. I want two dedicated groups to secure those once we break into the living quarter.'

'I will organise the groups, my King, and I will secure those stores for you.' Boen is quick to offer up his services.

'No, you and your plate-clad fighters must remain as my spear tip.' Teshu points at the boss of the brawlers. 'Rool and his infiltrators can do that.'

Rool gives a bow. 'Won't fail you, my King.'

A guard enters the house. 'I beg your forgiveness for this intrusion, my King.'

'If your reason is valid, then I'll grant it.'

The guard steps aside and yells at the door. 'Bring her in!'

Four more guards enter with an elderly female elf in their midst, her long wooden staff tapping on the floor as she walks.

'What is this all about?' Teshu places his hand on the hilt of his sword as the new arrival approaches the sand table.

'She talks of being able to aid us, my King.' The first guard delivers the line with a slightly raised tone to hide the fear of being flogged for interrupting his ruler.

The king smiles. 'You speak elven?'

'No, he does not. But I speak your language.'

'Well now. This is a pleasant surprise. An elf who is fluent in Trollish.' Teshu folds his arms, clearly impressed. 'Tell me, you worn-out old baby maker, how come you are so versed in my language?'

'Knew a Troll once.'

The king notices that the guards are still standing there. 'You're free to go back to your post. None shall be flogged for this. Go scoot.'

They bow in unison and leave.

'I'll speak with you in private.' The elf's voice is stern, betraying the fact that she has dealt with powerful figures all her life.

'If you must. But I'm curious if you have decided to sacrifice yourself in order to get close to me and put a blade between my ribs, a final act committed out of desperation.' Teshu taps the pommel of his sword. 'I've got it on good authority that you old elves like to do that, and I'm also aware of the fact that I don't know your name.'

'Those in Kutees call me Rhonda.'

'And I'm King to you.' Teshu claps his hands. 'Search her. Make sure she isn't packing anything sharper than her tongue.' He smiles at the elf. 'You understand it's just a formality.'

'I understand.' She lays her walking stick down and holds her arms up to be petted down.

The fighting bosses show no restraint as they grope her in inappropriate places to check for any concealed weapons; one even goes so far as to look down her top, much to the dismay of his king.

'Oi, fellar. That's uncalled for.' Teshu slaps the archery boss for having gone too far. 'Get out of here before I have you lashed.'

The boss gives a very low bow. 'Ask your forgiveness, my King. Humble ask.'

'Not given. Get back to the model.' Teshu gives the old elf a slight shrug. 'Apologies for that one. His mother didn't give him enough breast as a babe, now he craves it from all.'

'No need. They're just overly eager to please. That is part of your culture.'

'You know us well.' The sarcasm is thick in his reply as he gestures towards the door beside the dais. 'Come to my... new den. We can speak there in secret.'

'I'm honoured. I get to see the once-private room of the chief and chieftess of Teen,' Rhonda rasps as she pics her walking staff up.

'Ah, but you have to leave that behind.'

She chucks it at a nearby wizard. 'That has a lot of value to me, keep it safe.'

'So, Rhonda the elf. What brings you to my door?' The king places his hand on a clay flask sat on the large table which takes up an entire wall of the bedroom.

She smiles. 'It's been a while since I drank troll-wyn. Is that from the red or the yellow grape?'

'Does it matter?' Teshu gives her a sidelong glance.

'It matters not for I enjoy both wyns equally. Right now, I'm in the mood for some of the white stuff.'

Teshu's smile turns into a grin. He pours some into a silver goblet for her. 'Enjoy, for this comes from my personal fermenters.'

Rhonda sips the drink, savouring the tang before swallowing. 'Been so long since I tasted that delicate bitterness.' When she opens her eyes she notices that the king is staring at her expectantly. 'Thank you for that trip to the days of my youth.'

'Glad to be of service.'

'The reason I came here is to offer to you my services, so to speak.'

'Oh?' Teshu is surprised by what he hears. 'And to what do I owe such pleasure?'

'Let's just say that I'm of value to you.'

Amused by the statement, Teshu clears his throat before he observes: 'Bold words, but you do look like you've seen quite a few winters exchange places with spring.'

'You're very direct. Never saw that in the last king... I suspect he was not your father.'

Teshu seems slightly annoyed by the remark, but his tone remains neutral. 'The old king died and left the ruling chair to his incompetent son who wanted to sate the hunger of his starving people by appealing to the gods. Gods who didn't listen.'

'And you can do better by declaring war on the land of the elves?'

'And you come to my door to betray your own kind. Seems that both of us have a grievance with *your* kind,' Teshu is quick to fire back.

'My grievance is personal. Not sure what yours is.'

The king straightens up. 'I see. A personal grievance. The troll you knew, he was more than a mere friend. A love interest perhaps?'

'My husband to be. I loved him with all my heart.'

Hands folded behind his back, Teshu walks around in a little circuit. 'But you were not liked for your choice, I suspect. Elves and trolls can't have offspring together, and having those is vital to the survival of any kingdom – no matter which name you ascribed to it.'

'If you must know, one male elf from the elven community in Four Villages came at my lover with a copper dagger and a club with a stone blade. Sliced him up really badly, then caved his skull in to make sure he was dead. Beat me to a pulp with his bare fists...' She lifts her tunic, exposing herself to reveal a thick old scar across her lower abdomen. 'Then he left an unwanted child in my belly. The shiguma cut it out at my behest.'

Teshu stops dead in his tracks when he sees the scar. 'I see. One male ruined your life. Why do you feel like you must punish all of your kin? This tale you shared with me, how long ago was that? Two hundred years, at the time of my father's father, my great-father?'

'Once again I find myself being ousted by my own people. By a chief who refuses to listen to me, a chief blinded by the sweet lips of those around him.' Along with spittle, bitterness pours out of her mouth.

'I brought almost all of my people here, thousands of fighters and thousands more who are close to fighting age. Our numbers outrank those of the elves trapped on the island by a great magnitude. So, I ask you again, what good are you to me?'

She walks over to the table, slams the goblet down and takes a seat on the floor, closing her eyes. 'I'll show, insolent child.'

Several wizards enter the den, their daggers drawn, but the king halts them in their tracks.

'Stay back. All is well here.'

Rhonda finishes her chant and opens her eyes, looking

straight at the leader of the trolls. He, along with the wizards, jumps back.

'Her eyes are glowing! Why are her eyes glowing!?' The scream comes from the wizard in charge of provisions.

Teshu grimaces at his advisor. 'Yell in my ear like that again and I'll have you flogged.'

'Beg your forgiveness, my King.'

'Get out, all of you. Leave me and the elf-wizard.' He shoves them back towards the main hall of the hut and slams the doors shut before he spins around and approaches the wytch. 'Why have I never heard of this magic before?'

'Because elves practice true magic. Trolls use the trickery of mixing substances together to emulate magic.'

He waves her comment off. 'Not that. I've read everything my people learned about you elves since they began keeping records, and yet none of the papyrus scrolls mention glowing eyes.'

She places a hand on the ground and pats it. 'Then you won't know of this.'

Several rats leap down out of the rafters onto the bed before scurrying over to the one who has summoned them, their eyes emitting the same glow. They do all sorts of tricks, depending on what the old wytch commands them to do. At the end of it all they stand on their hind legs and give a slight bow to the king before Rhonda releases the rats, allowing them to scurry away.

Teshu gets on all fours and crawls closer. 'That was... amazing. Do all elves possess this power?'

'Not all.' Rhonda smiles, elated to see a king grovel before her. 'Everyone has some sort of magical ability or sensitivity. It is rare for elves to be born blunt. Some, like the little sow who's taken my place, have three... perhaps four talents. She could become a danger later on.'

Teshu pats the elderly elf's hand and looks her in the eyes as if he was falling in love with her. 'Just like that, Fonolite places the greatest gift in my hands.' He leans over and kisses her on the cheek. 'You shall have your revenge and I shall reclaim the lands of my god and my ancestors. Together we shall right the ancient wrongs and the world shall thank us.'

Amused by his excitement Rhonda smiles at him and declares: 'You must understand that I have limited range on how far I can reach out and how many animals I can control.'

'Can you control any animal?'

'I can, because their minds are simple and easily overwhelmed.'

Suddenly the king lies down on the floor and rests his head in her lap. 'We'll figure something out. Something that will make the best use of your abilities.'

Rhonda strokes the king's fine black hair; the moment is stirring up an old memory. 'There is one particular animal I want to use to aid you.'

'There is?'

Her voice has turned unusually gentle. 'Those from the Bruveen village call him Halfmoon.'

HARVESTING TOUR

Four figures cramped into a hollowed-out cedar trunk row across the river. It is still dark and the sun is a long way from rising. Sat at the back of the dugout is Jakka, Keties' most experienced hunter; he mimics a cough to keep the others paddling in unison, making it easier for them to work together against the fast-flowing waters. Blisteringly cold winds blowing from the northeast hurt their fingers and cause their muscles to seize up, but they persevere for they have no other choice.

All four members of the harvesting party are travelling light: The two wytches have armed themselves with recurve bows while the hunters have brought a spear and a short sword each. They are dressed in double-layered tunics and trousers. Halfway across the river it starts to snow again, a deluge that drops visibility down to arm's length.

'Oh, what a blessing,' Jakka comments between his time keeping coughs; no one can tell if he is being serious or sarcastic because of his heavy southern accent.

Yelqen decides to test the atmosphere. 'Well, it'll make us harder to spot when we touch the other bank.'

'It will. Hence why I said blessing. I hope your wife is right about this meadow we're going to.' Jakka's muses with his signature rolling of the R.

Isfael realises that he is being sarcastic but remains silent and keeps paddling while the Keties hunter steers the dugout towards a small creek. Once ashore they flip their transport over, drag it under a bunch of overhanging branches and hide their oars underneath the hollowed-out trunk.

'Hope the trolls are too stupid to notice the sudden appearance of large log here,' Farnu says while unslinging her bow.

'We can only hope.' Isfael also takes her bow off her shoulder and tucks it under her thin tunic to keep it dry.

Jakka, who has the same dark brown skin as the chief of his village, gestures for them to close in. 'All good to go?'

They nod.

'Right. Northeast, you say?' He directs his question at the Bravin wytch.

'Yes, for about thirty miles.'

The Keties hunter gives a grunt. 'Right. We head into the wind. Best I can do in terms of trekking, seeing as how we don't have the sun or the stars to guide us.' He taps his mouth with his index finger. 'We must be very quiet now. Follow me, stay close.'

As no one can offer up an alternative method of navigation or add anything of worth to the conversation they set off in silence.

The snowfall, which gets worse with every step the small party takes, counts in their favour since it muffles their movement. Jakka is forced to change direction a few times as they keep running into the enemy outposts. A lack of proper winter clothing has forced the trolls to make fire; they chat loudly and make jokes, clearly not expecting anyone to try and sneak through their lines in the middle of what has become a snowstorm.

None of the elves are insane enough to try and attack any of the small encampments because they have been placed within earshot of each other, and sneaking past the trolls is much easier than they had anticipated. Jakka makes a mental note of the lacklustre encirclement; he is adamant that he will report this to the chief upon his return. He whispers this intent to Yelqen, asking him to fulfil the tasks should he not make it back. The Bravin hunter agrees.

All night long they continue on their journey, following the wildlife trails through the thick forest. On several occasions they are forced to backtrack because the undergrowth has either collapsed under the weight of the snow or the animals stopped using a particular track, allowing the plants to reclaim the precious spit of land.

Jakka's pace is slow as he is effectively navigating blind. When he suddenly stops and gets his weapon ready the others do the same.

Yelqen approaches him. 'What is it?'

'Do you smell it?'

He sniffs the air and is hit by a pungent odour of old urine. 'Blaiff pissing post. But I don't sense any of them nearby.'

'Have you got a talent for such things?' Jakka asks while contemplating their next move.

'I do indeed. It reaches out quite far.'

'Good, keep feeling our surroundings, because that amount of stink would suggest that we're in the territory of a large pack.'

Acutely aware of the dangers that a pack of blaiffs could present to the harvesting party, Isfael is not only scared but also mad at herself. In an attempt to control her fear, she sarcastically remarks: 'Wonderful, I've just laid the table for a bunch of two-legged wolves.'

'Don't get disheartened now, young wytch.' Jakka tries to sound encouraging, but his tone comes across as mocking. 'We keep the noise low and we'll make it through, still breathing the air of this world and not that of the afterlife.' He nods to himself. 'Yes, straight on is the best course for now. Come.'

The dawn draws near and the snowfall tapers off slightly. Yelqen notices the perfect spot for them to camp under a cluster of fir trees packed so tightly they prevent the snow from reaching the ground. The other three are incredibly grateful for the rest break.

Jakka is quick to get a small fire going. 'There. We've put some distance between us and the enemy. Any troll this far out is definitely lost.'

Yelqen squats down behind his wife wraps his arms around her to keep her warm. 'How much further do you think, my dear?'

'We've been going at a fair pace. Perhaps we'll get there in another few hours. That's unless everyone here wants to get some shuteye.'

'Not me.' Farnu takes a pouch out of her shoulder bag. 'We drink this, and we'll be good to go till evening.'

Isfael holds her hand out. 'What sort of mix is that?'

Farnu hands over the pouch which filled to the brim with powdered plant material. 'Dried rhodiolrosea stems, gottuhola seeds, ashwaga buds, bacoppa roots and peppermint. All ground up and mixed together. Drink this and you'll be good as new.'

Isfael sticks the tip of her finger in and tries the concoction. 'Wooo. That is bitter.' She hands the pouch back. 'Not heard of such a concoction before. What ratios do you use to stop those plants poisoning you?'

'It's a recipe of my own and it works.' Farnu pours the powder into a small silver cup and places it beside the fire. 'I'll write it down for you once we get back.'

'Appreciated, thank you.' Isfael leans into her husband's embrace, enjoying his closeness.

'What good is knowledge when kept to ourselves, eh?' Farnu winks at the other wytch.

'Peppermint helps to perk you up?' Yelqen sounds a bit dubious.

'A bit, yes, but I suspect she adds it to hide the extreme bitterness of the other plants.' Isfael pats her husband's hand while explaining her understanding of the mixture.

'Indeed. Without peppermint, this stuff will make your tongue jump out of your mouth.'

All of a sudden Yelqen pushes his wife away and gets into a fighting stance, spear ready. 'We're being watched.'

Jakka also gets to his feet, ready to fight. 'Can you say how many?'

'One… no, more joining… the watcher. Powerful. He's drawing near.' Yelqen turns and faces the path they have been following. 'There, roughly twelve… or maybe fifteen beasts.'

An enormous grey blaiff steps out of the dark forest, its bright yellow eyes lingering on each of the elves. At eight and half feet, the wolf is easily two heads taller than all of them, and its thick winter pelt hides a muscular frame. The pack patriarch who is scouting ahead of his family circles the group cowering beneath the densely packed trees before letting out a huff and clicking the long black claws of its index finger and thumb together. After a short moment a similar sound comes out of the darkness and a female blaiff steps into the light. She is equal in stature to the male, except that her pelt is black as night and her eyes are more green than yellow.

One by one the rest of the pack come into view, all of them sparing the elves sidelong glances on their way past. A young male moves closer to Isfael and sniffs at her hands; it brings a smile to her face, but she is careful not to show any teeth. The mother of the curious cub grabs him by the scruff and shoves him back in line with a growl. Not wanting to draw the ire of an animal that can kill her with one blow Isfael lowers her gaze.

One by one the pack vanishes into the forest again, the last member to disappear being the patriarch who watched over his family.

'That was exciting!' Isfael turns to face her companions, a wide grin on her face.

Farnu quickly pulls the cup away from the fire. 'Dammit. Not sure if this got too hot and ruined the brew.'

'Make another.' Jakka sits down again, smiling at the Bravin wytch. 'If our trip shows us that there's no meadow, then at least we have an interesting tale to share around the hearths.'

Farnu gets the cup far enough away from the fire and packs it with snow to cool it down. 'I can't make another brew. I've brought enough to give everyone a single boost but not more.'

Yelqen takes some provisions out and sits down close to the

fire. 'Well, either way, we'll get this done. With or without that concoction.'

'Oh, yes,' says Farnu and takes a sip before she continues, 'it didn't get too hot after all. Here, young wytch, try this.'

Isfael takes the cup in both hands and sips the concoction. 'Ooof. Tastes like pitch.'

'That's what you want. Means it is good. One mouthful should keep you going for most of the day.'

As soon as Yelqen has had his share he pulls a face and retches as if he was going to vomit. 'By Father Welkin's sweaty sack, that is vile. So this stuff will keep you going even if you haven't slept?'

'Even then.'

Jakka takes a sip. 'Hmm, wish I'd had this on all those long hunts I went on in my youth. Would've brought home twice as many pounds of flesh.' He grimaces at the aftertaste. 'Or perhaps not. I would've been gagging too loud!'

The others laugh at the silly jest and move a little closer to the fire as the wind picks up.

ANCIENT BEAST

High above the world the parting clouds allow the sun to shine through and make the land unbearably bright. All four elves squint and shield their eyes at the sudden change. With the increase in temperature clumps of snow slide off the branches, hitting the forest floor with wet squelches.

'Dammit.' Jakka digs the slush out of his neck. 'I hate it when the snow lands there.'

Isfael pulls her tunic up against her neck. 'Got to love the late autumn weather.'

'Indeed.' Yelqen sounds uncomfortable.

The other three stop and look at him.

When he notices their attention he comes to a halt. 'What?'

'Are you sensing something?' Isfael is on edge; by her reckoning they should have already reached the clearing.

'Hmm... I can pick up a presence, but I'm not sure what it is.'

Jakka, who looks around to see if he can spot anything, discovers a patch of green among the white and dark grey of the wintery landscape. 'Well, that is something you don't see every day.' He begins walking again and quickly realises that they have arrived. 'Well done, young wytch. You were right.'

Isfael forgets about her husband's unease and runs to the edge of the clearing. 'This is amazing.' Spread out before them is a green meadow with a handful of orchard trees scattered throughout, all of them swarmed by flies that are feasting on the sugar of the overripe fruits they shed. It is a fantastic sight to behold, but as something doesn't feel right she backs away. 'This is wrong, and I don't mean this slice of summer in the heart of cold and snow.'

'What could be so wrong? Look at all the medicine plants swaying in the wind,' says Fanru who can't believe her eyes.

'That's just it. Why are there no grazers making the best of this bounty? Why is that blaiff pack not here basking in the sun?' Isfael nods to herself. 'The legends of a dragon must be real.'

'The beast can't be here anymore. I saw those records and they were written three or so generations back.' Farnu's voice betrays her eagerness to get harvesting.

'Maybe that the dragon is immortal. Or there is more than one. Perhaps they're a family that keep coming back here, waiting for fools like us to wander into the open so they can pounce.' Isfael nods to herself again. 'But we have to risk it. We have to if we're to help the village.'

Jakka lowers his stance. 'I'll go first. See what is what.'

Farnu faces the Bravin hunter. 'Can't you sense anything?'

'No, not really,' Yelqen replies and shakes his head before he continues, 'I can sense a few animals, but they're far off. Skittish. As for the rage of a predator, that I can't feel.' He looks off into the distance. 'I do feel something that could be described as pleasure or joy, perhaps. It is a bizarre feeling.'

'But no danger,' Farnu presses.

'No, none of the anticipation-fear that I would feel if a dangerous predator would be watching us.'

The Keties hunter steps onto the green grass of the clearing and hunkers down, his eyes observing the snow-covered tree line. 'If we keep low, we might avoid the creature's gaze. Let the grass hide us.'

'That's actually a brilliant idea,' agrees Yelqen, impressed by the other hunter's logic and somewhat surprised that he didn't think of it.

Isfael gets onto all fours and crawls over to the nearest thing she can harvest. 'No point standing around thinking about it. We'll just have to take the risk.'

'I'm with you there.' Yelqen follows his wife.

Farnu gets down and crawls over to her fellow villager. 'We'll go a little bit further along. That way we'll cover more ground.'

'Good thinking.'

Both wytches are elated by the overabundance of the fresh growth and their harvest sacks fill up with usable plants very quickly. Yelqen remains a few paces behind his wife, shuffling along on all fours and rising up on one knee, constantly checking for danger and looking over at the other hunter to see whether they have spotted anything.

Isfael is about to harvest a plant with her copper sickle when she notices movement on the far side of the clearing, roughly three hundred feet away; it is unlike any other forest creature she has ever seen. Looking back, she can see her husband who has also spotted the beast and is now desperately trying to draw the other two's attention by throwing little stones at them.

At first Jakka seems annoyed by the pebble that bounces off his shoulder, but he quickly realises what is going on when the dragon is pointed out to him. Scrambling over, he gets Farnu to hunker down in the long grass, letting her know that they have to be quiet.

All four of them are now focused on the opposite side of the clearing, searching for anything that seems out of place. Isfael picks up on the creature's movement again and tracks it as it walks along the edge of the forest, staying just within the tree line.

Suddenly, without warning, the animal steps into the light and sniffs the air, giving all four elves a very good look at it. Striding on two legs, the dragon is about twice the size of a horse and covered in off-white feathers. A thin line of red feathers starts behind its eye and runs the length of its body, terminating at the tip of its long muscular tail. Using its front claws it flips a fallen tree trunk over with relative ease, a sight that makes Isfael's heart skip a beat because it betrays the beast's true potential.

Once again the dragon raises its olive-shaped head to sniff the air, letting out a low rumble that makes the very air reverberate. It strides along the edge of the clearing for a bit before it disappears into the forest again, seemingly unaware of the elves that have entered into its domain.

Yelqen whispers to his wife: 'Time we left.'

She nods while crawling back; her heart thumping gains her ribs. 'I do agree with you there.'

A little further along the other two are also making their way off the meadow and into the trees, hoping that the vegetation will provide them with some sort of protection.

Yelqen stops just short of the tree line when a feeling of overwhelming joy slams up against his mind, followed by a heart wrenching realisation. 'It's all backwards. These things think in the opposite direction.'

Isfael is about to ask what he is talking about when they hear a low roar. Where the Keties couple were last seen they watch a second dragon stride into the clearing with the hunter firmly gripped in its front claws. Jakka stabs the huge beast in its arm with his fighting dagger, but his defiance is short-lived as his head is bitten off and swallowed in one snap of the powerful jaws. Farnu loses off one arrow after another, sending them into the animal's flank, but its thick feathers prevent them from doing any significant damage. When it drops the headless corpse and spits a blob of bright yellow at the Keties wytch; Farnu's blood-curdling scream cuts through the air as her face and chest melt away.

Yelqen shoves his wife. 'Go now!'

'Her bag...'

Without hesitation he grabs her arm and drags her along. 'Don't care! Move!'

They run as fast as they can, holding their hands up to deflect the branches. The trees rush past, old branches under the snow crack and pop with each footfall. Heat trapped by winter clothing makes them break out in a sweat, but they don't stop running.

Exhausted by the long sprint through the forest they eventually come to a halt and hunker down amongst a bunch of fallen trees to catch their breath. Neither says a word, their eyes skirting around to look for danger. Slowly their hearts simmer down and their heaving chests return to normal. Closely followed by his wife, Yelqen gets up and moves to a different location where they hide amongst the shrubbery again and wait to see if anything has run them down.

Isfael checks whether her bag, which she stuffed full of precious plant material in the meadow, has been torn open during the sprint, but to her delight it has held up. Next she addresses her husband: 'We need to get our bearings.'

'We can worry about directions later. For now, we need to get away.'

She wipes the sweat off her face. 'Records spoke of one dragon, not a pair.'

'Either way they'll be stalking us.' Yelqen reaches out with his senses. 'Backwards thinking. I must feel for... pleasure. Joy in hunting... no the fear of failure of injury.' After a few counts he relinquishes the search. 'I can't sense them. These buggers are slippery.'

Her face drops slightly. 'Dammit. Dammit!'

'Calm down, we'll get out of here alive. We just need to be sensible about our next move.'

Isfael thinks for a moment. 'I'm certain that these dragons can see at night. Best not be in the area when the sun goes down.'

'Hopefully the beasts will remain close to the nice warm lawn instead of chasing us into the freezing cold forest.' She checks her bag again and then ties the opening shut with some cord. 'Good, I've not lost any of the harvest and I'm not planning to do so later.'

Yelqen steps out of their hiding spot, spear ready. 'I'll take the lead.'

'And I'll keep an eye on the back.' Isfael unslings her bow and sets an arrow in place.

When they find a well-used deer path they decide to follow it. Judging by the direction of the wind they are not quite going in the right direction, but anywhere far away from the clearing is good enough for now. Neither elf pays much attention to the sky becoming overcast and the light snowfall dusting the world around them.

A thought stirs in Yelqen's mind that turns from a feeling of intense desire into a sensation that halts him in his tracks: bloodlust. The intoxicating need to consume flesh makes his head spin as it indicates that they are in mortal danger. As he abruptly stops, Isfael draws her bow; she is ready for the fight.

One of the dragons bursts out of a thicket, its long strides powering it towards the delicious morsel, its four-fingered claws outstretched, ready to dig into flesh. Yelqen sees the beast bearing down on his wife and pushes her to safety while simultaneously thrusting at the open maw with his spear. The sharpened bronze tip punches through the soft flesh at the back of the throat, forcing the creature to snap its head up to try and avoid the pain, but the dragon's momentum carries it along and causes it to trample the elf with its powerful legs.

Even though the awkward manner in which she has landed has knocked her wind out, Isfael manages to get up and shoots a couple of arrows at the dragon as it staggers away before she realises that her husband is lying very still. 'Yelqen?' Her voice is low and fearful. 'Yelqen? Are you hurt?'

A moan creeps over his lips, a moan she heard before, when her grandfather was crushed by a boat mast. Just like that day, the sound fills her with dread. 'No! Please, Nammu, not this.' She drops her bow and goes to his side. 'Yelqen, please tell me you're not hurt.'

He turns his head towards her and tries to smile, but his face is contorted in a mask of pain; a trickle of blood flows out of his nose, his teeth covered in a thin red film. 'Issee... run.'

'No, no! I'm not leaving you here.'

'Rhhuuunn... save yourself.' His voice is weak, his breath

shallow.

Somewhere in the darkness of the forest the dragon lets out a pained roar, followed by a loud whine akin to a yelping dog.

Yelqen tries to lift his arm. 'Run... save yourself, save our daughter.'

She pulls her axe out for the off chance that she might need it to defend them while uttering the chant that'll give her the healer sight. 'I'm getting you back to Keties. Just give me...' She stops talking when she sees the extent of her husband's injuries. 'No, Nammu, no.'

'Go... run. I'm already dead...'

Isfael wants to tell him not to give up so quickly, but her eyes have shown her all the broken bones and torn muscles; she knows he will not make it. 'I can get you home. I just need to make a litter to drag you.'

'No. Leave. Please.'

'*Ogllot helps,*' the voice in the gem utters, clear as day.

'Not now, Ogllot,' she replies without thinking about it.

'Go, save our babe.' Yelqen urges his wife to leave.

The dragon roars again, this time much closer than before, and much angrier.

'*Ogllot helps. Use jewel.*'

'Dammit, Ogllot, not now!' Isfael moves over to a fallen tree and begins to hack at its branches.

Another roar, then a howl.

'*Use jewel. Save the life!*'

'I said not now!'

'Run, save yourself, save the child.'

The axe glances off a branch, slamming into her thigh. 'Ow! Dammit!'

A pained howl erupts from the forest before several snarls are heard; it is the blaiff pack. Another powerful roar, another yelping wolf.

'*Use jewel, stupid elf. Save the life!*'

Isfael scream at her harvest sack. 'Shut up! Let me do my work!'

'You must leave!' Yelqen insists.

'*USE JEWEL!*' Ogllot's voice barrels into her mind, forcing her to stagger back and hold her head.

'Stop! Just stop!' she screams at the bag again. 'You're going to kill me if you do that again.'

'Isfael, please go, run.' Yelqen tries to crawl towards his wife, but he lacks the strength to do so.

'*Then hear Ogllot you must!*'

Eventually Isfael stows her axe and moves to her husband's side. 'Shhh. Stay still.'

'You… stubborn female. Leave me… here.'

A young blaiff staggers out of the forest, its left arm missing along with half of its muzzle.

When Isfael sees the beast she decides to place her trust in the person trapped in the gem. 'How can you help us, Ogllot?'

'*Elf must to take jewel. Put to head of husband. Tell life of husband to enter jewel. Use of you power to move life.*'

'Who… is… Gollhott?' Yelqen's eyes roll back in his head before returning to normal.

'He's a friend. Don't speak.' She thinks about the words for a moment. 'So I force his soul into the gem.'

'*Use of you power…*'

'Use my magic – yes, I understand the idea, but how do I put it into practice?'

A female blaiff runs out of the forest and grabs hold of the dying male, desperately trying to pull him to his feet, but to no avail.

'Shit. shit.' Isfael presses the stone to her husband's forehead and whispers: 'I command your soul to enter the gem.'

'Run… you must… run,' Yelqen sounds weaker with each breath.

'I command your soul to enter the gem.' This time she tries to be more forceful.

'*Life of him not come!*'

Isfael tries to visualise a soul leaving the body and being absorbed by the gem.

'Life of him not come!'

Several blaiffs burst out of the forest. The female abandons the dying male and runs after her fellows. They sprint past the elves and vanish among the trees. Isfael can hear something large push its way through the undergrowth and come straight towards her.

Desperate to save her husband's life she visualises pushing him off a cliff. 'I command you to enter this damn jewel.' As an image of her unborn child flashes through her mind she doubles over.

Powerful contractions grip her stomach and lower back, reaching down between her legs. The muscles pull together with so much force that it feels to her as if they would tear themselves to shreds. Unbearable pain causes Isfael to scream, releasing a shockwave that destroys the trees around her before she drops to the ground unconscious.

AFTERLIFE

A weak sun breaks through the clouds, its light causing Isfael to squint. Slowly, very slowly she tries to sit up, but her muscles refuse to obey. She is forced to roll onto her front and get up on all fours before she can manage a sitting position.

Her immediate surroundings are devoid of snow and plant growth. She stares at the clearing, confused by why she is there and what may have caused the lack of vegetation. About twenty paces away she sees a figure dangling in a tree. Something about it is familiar. When she tries to stand up she finds that her stomach muscles are incapable of helping her achieve that goal. She has to rock back and forth to try and use her momentum, but no sooner has she got to her feet when everything goes black and a flash of unbearable pain shoots up through her thighs, guts and chest.

Too weak to try again she lies back down and gathers her thoughts. Then a shockwave rocks her body and makes her tremble as a terrible thought creeps up on her: The figure dangling in the tree is her husband, her beloved Yelqen, the elf that matters most to her, the father of her unborn child.

'Yelqen! Yelqen!' she calls out to him, each syllable accompanied by an unbearable pain that punches her in the guts. She rolls onto her back and begins to cry, unable to bear it any longer. 'Yelqen, please answer me.'

No answer comes. The only sounds she hears is the wind

blowing through the branches.

Suddenly another realisation dawns on her and she reaches between her legs. When she pulls her hand back and sees the blood on her fingers, she pleads: 'No, this can't be... Please, Mother Nammu, not my child.'

Something approaches, an animal of some kind.

Isfael ignores the sound as she once again tries to get to her feet. 'No, please. Not my husband and my child, please, dear Mother.' Her sobs and cries are snatched away by the wind. 'No, please.'

A clawed hand grabs hold of her shoulder and pulls her into a sitting position. Looking down at her is large female blaiff with golden green eyes and behind the female is the patriarch.

Isfael pulls her arms tight against her chest. 'Please make it quick. Don't make me suffer any more.'

The female wolf picks her up and, for the first time, the young wytch can see beyond the small depression where she has lain unconscious. On the edge of the perfectly circular clearing is the headless body of a dragon, most of its guts eaten away by the blaiffs. The powerful arms of the matriarch fill the elf with a slither of comfort, despite the uncertainty of what the future holds. Resting in Isfael's palm is a gem, a stone that is more valuable to her than life.

To be continued...

Printed in Great Britain
by Amazon

22826734R00118